PENGUIN BOOKS

THE MAPS OF CAMARINES

Maryanne Moll has written three books. Her first book, *Awakenings* (2001), and her second book, *Little Freedoms* (2003), are both collections of essays. Her third book, *Married Women* (2014), is a short story collection, and the book was a finalist for the Cirilo F. Bautista Prize for Best Book of Short Fiction in English in 2014. Her short story 'At Merienda' won Third Prize in the 2005 Don Carlos Palanca Memorial Awards for Literature.

Maryanne's short stories have also been included in anthologies, which includes *Philippine Speculative Fiction IV*, *Philippine Genre Stories: Special Crime Edition*, and *Anomalous 30*. She was a fellow for the National Writer's Workshops in the University of Santo Tomas (2002), Dumaguete (2002), and the University of the Philippines (2021). Before writing fiction, she was a reporter and columnist for *Bikol Daily*, and also worked as disk jockey and newscaster for an FM radio station in Naga City, Camarines Sur. She has created and managed some publications for the Philippine National Police. More recently, she has worked as a Publications Specialist for a government-owned-and-controlled corporation for more than ten years.

She has earned units for the degree Master of Arts in Creative Writing at the University of the Philippines Diliman, before transferring to a different degree programme. She is currently working on her thesis for Master of Arts in Comparative Literature, Major in Literary Theory, at the UP Diliman.

The Maps of Camarines

a novel

Maryanne Moll

PENGUIN BOOKS
An imprint of Penguin Random House

PENGUIN BOOKS

USA | Canada | UK | Ireland | Australia
New Zealand | India | South Africa | China | Southeast Asia

Penguin Books is part of the Penguin Random House group of companies
whose addresses can be found at global.penguinrandomhouse.com

Published by Penguin Random House SEA Pte Ltd
9, Changi South Street 3, Level 08-01,
Singapore 486361

Penguin
Random House
SEA

First published in Penguin Books by Penguin Random House SEA 2023

This is a work of fiction, and although some of the historical details pertaining
to the Philippines are real, the place names of Toog, Kamansi and Mangkono
are completely fictional. Furthermore, although the place called Camarines
evokes the old Ambos Camarines, it is not meant to represent the current
Camarines Sur or Camarines Norte.

ISBN 9789815058901

Typeset in Adobe Calson Pro by MAP Systems, Bengaluru, India

www.penguin.sg

For my two grandmothers, Francisca Kare viuda de Moll and
Mariquita Garchitorena Remo

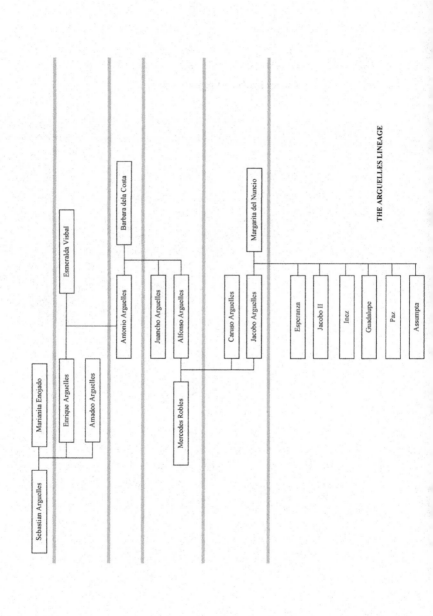

THE ARGUELLES LINEAGE

Contents

Chapter 1

The Children

Assumpta Arguelles was born at five minutes past midnight, one day after the Feast of the Assumption, in the year 1949. Her mother, Margarita del Nuncio, was already past her forties and had given birth to six other children prior. One of the children died when he was seven, after contracting complications from polio. After Assumpta was born, Margarita swore to her husband Jacobo Arguelles that this daughter would be the last, and that she would no longer allow her husband to sleep in her bedroom from then on. Jacobo, a man who had been raised by a family of Arguelles matriarchs who used the centuries to perfect the art of pushing their men around, simply nodded in agreement.

Jacobo was a quiet man, set in his ways, but his ways were not his own. As the seasons of planting and harvesting in the vast Arguelles lands dictated the progress of his days, so did his wife dictate the time of his waking, eating and sleeping. When she prohibited him from sleeping in her bedroom, he did not tell her that he preferred to sleep alone in his own bedroom and that he never really liked sleeping in her bedroom when he was required to. He had actually always preferred, since the beginning of their marriage, to lull himself to sleep in his own bed while reading novels, rather than allow himself to be lulled to sleep by his wife, in bed, complaining about the latest antics of the servants.

As is the habit of couples who have been sharing years of life and death and darkness together, they kept secrets from each other. They had to do this just to be able to stand each other's presence in the same house and keep the union alive. With Margarita's verdict, Jacobo was thankful to have to keep one less secret from his wife. He became even quieter.

Assumpta grew up as her father's favourite and was given the run of the entire house. This included Jacobo's vast library of the classics, manuscripts and monographs of geography, politics and theology. The library also held a vast range of huge, very old maps kept in a tall and wide chest, with drawers so shallow that only up to seven maps could lie perfectly flat inside each one. No map was ever the same, and some of the lines and writings on the older maps had already faded through time, the edges of the paper crumbling through Assumpta's small, pudgy fingers. In the imaginings of her seven-year-old mind, these were the worlds that existed before she did, and their maps have faded because the worlds have already disappeared from reality. Those maps that could still be read are worlds that still exist, where people still live, and have not yet dissipated into thin air. She mentioned this idea once to Paz, her older sister, then nine-years-old, who called her crazy.

Assumpta was closest to Paz, because they shared the same bedroom and the same nanny and the same tutor, and on the night that she told this idea to Paz, there was a thunderstorm.

'Paz,' Assumpta whispered loudly through the strong winds whistling through the cracks in the windows and joints of the house.

'What?' Paz murmured through her blankets, her nose and mouth covered, her dark eyes half-shut, looking at Assumpta.

'I think I know how to find out which world is going to disappear next.'

'What are you talking about?' Paz's half-shut eyes still managed to roll a little bit.

'The maps. The maps,' Assumpta was more excited now, her voice becoming a little louder as the wind outside howled more forcibly.

'The maps? In Papa's chest of drawers?'

'Yes. Those maps. I've seen them all.'

'Why did you even bother?' Paz said, throwing her blankets off her body and propping her head up on her headboard. 'They are so dusty. I looked at them once and they made me sneeze, and I never opened those drawers again. And Papa doesn't let me into the library as often, anyway.'

'But I know the secret of the maps,' Assumpta said, in a very loud whisper over the sound of the rain.

'What secret?' Paz started to sound frustrated.

'The maps tell us which worlds are going to disappear next.' Assumpta knew she rarely had an audience in Paz, so she was taking advantage of this moment.

'What? What worlds? You mean like other countries?'

'No, other worlds.' Assumpta sat up.

Paz sat up as well. 'I have no idea what you're talking about. Mrs Palacio said there is only one Earth. Are we going to disappear?'

'No, there's not just us. There are other worlds,' Assumpta said, gesticulating with her hands and arms. 'We can't see them because many of them have already disappeared.' Then, dissatisfied with her gesticulation, she stood up and used her entire body to demonstrate to Paz what she was trying to explain. 'When a world is created, a map of it is made. When the map fades away, so does that world, and all the people who live in it.' Assumpta swept her arms dramatically towards the window and the wet darkness beyond it. 'They no longer exist. They're just … gone,' she even paused before saying the final word with an ominous tone.

'That's just crazy,' Paz scoffed. 'If you tell Mrs Palacio that, she will think you're crazy too. Better keep it a secret.' And then Paz laid back in her bed, turned her back to Assumpta, hid under her blankets once more, and fell silent.

Assumpta lay awake for some time after that, thinking through her theory, while the rain fell in torrents outside. She wondered about the people in those worlds and how they disappeared. Did they just fall asleep and fade into the air? What about their houses? Did they just fade away like the lines on the maps faded away? Did they burn to the ground? Did the trees sink into the deep soil of the forests? She wondered about these other worlds, which, by all the capabilities of her faculties, were real for a time, until she grew up and discovered that things were not that simple.

She fell asleep shortly before dawn once the rain had died down, exhausted by all the worlds that her mind had wandered to. She rose joyfully to sunshine and anticipation of a hearty, warm breakfast.

Of course Paz forgot about the entire conversation the very next morning, and Assumpta never told anyone else about her idea about the maps ever again. And that was how, at seven-years-old, at the birth of her very first secret, Assumpta was inducted into the Arguelleses's long-standing family tenet that secrets were necessary for life and for the world to go on as destined.

And just like all other seven-year-old girls who believe they have uncovered a profound secret, Assumpta secretly persevered in her exploration of the maps and the other papers in Jacobo's library. She was just learning how to read long words, and the strange-looking handwriting was barely decipherable to her. Nevertheless, she still persisted in studying the maps, noticing the dates—those, at least, she could make out—and the differences in the territorial lines, the shifts the seams in between certain land masses.

She could not read all of them yet, because the old style of print writing ended in upstrokes that she was not accustomed to. However, she took notice of the names of places that she could read and perceived several changes in the names. She was, of course, too young to understand the strategic implications of these, nor could she read the names of the owners, written in ancient cursive, on some maps, that would have shed light on everything she found mysterious about the entire matter. She had a secret and she was free to pursue it, so she did, but told no one else, not even Paz this time.

Seven-year-old Assumpta ponderously put her secret in the safest possible place in her heart. She swore to herself that she would make it her mission in life to make sense of it someday, while continuing to roam the rooms and halls of the great house and study the stories that the lines on the maps seemed to tell her.

Meanwhile, Esperanza, the eldest, then approaching eighteen, was incessantly preoccupied with things of little consequence in the greater scheme of things, but which meant the whole universe to girls of her age and social stature. She was obsessed with boys and dresses and shoes and hairstyles. She got excited about jewellery and soirees. The highlight of some of her days were the chatty letters brought by chauffeurs and envoys from her friends' house to hers, which she read while squeaking and giggling and jumping around.

When the telephone came to Camarines, she pestered her father to no end, until Jacobo, used to the political and emotional power that women—including his daughters—had over him, finally had one installed in the living room. As far as anyone else knew, no one used that telephone but Esperanza. And when she was not in the living room, talking on the telephone for hours, she spent most of her days in her bedroom. Sometimes she was in front of her dresser, assiduously verifying that her carefully plucked eyebrows were always perfectly symmetrical. Sometimes she was on the rug on the floor with sheets of paper and a pencil and an assortment of crayons, designing outfits and accessories for her upcoming eighteenth birthday.

She, of course, wanted to be the most beautiful girl in the most magnificent gown on that evening that she would claim as her own and no one else's. She expected herself to be wearing the most important jewellery of the Arguelleses, worn by a long line of Arguelles-blooded women to their own debuts and weddings and soirees with important political and historical figures. She saw her predecessors wearing the most beautiful finery when attending reunions with old families of similar calibre, like the Visbales and the Monsantillos, themselves all owners of vast lands in Camarines, and foresaw herself becoming like them soon. She often daydreamt about her official entrance to society: her guests rising at her appearance, spellbound at her beauty and grace, dumbstruck at the elegance of her dress and the way she carried herself as she walked down the hall to the ballroom, mesmerized by the queenly way she wore the jewellery of her matriarchs.

The other Arguelles daughter, Inez, was only fourteen and cared more for horses and their father's harvests. She followed their brother, Jacobo II, like a shadow, instead of beginning her task to understand the necessary and proper accoutrements of an Arguelles lady's life. Inez was a stark contrast to Esperanza, and the older girl felt rather surprised that there was such a girl-creature like Inez and that their parents actually allowed her such behaviour. However, Esperanza just ignored her boorish sister with her sun-kissed skin and the scars on her arms and her legs, and instead shared her ladylike daydreams and details of her life only with her closest friend, Sofia Monsantillo.

Esperanza loved the weekends, when she could do all of these things, and stay in bed and have her breakfast served there, and read romance novels and fashion magazines. She would sometimes visit with Sofia on warm, balmy afternoons, sitting on their porches and drinking lemonade and eating fruit tarts, talking about boys, or riding their bicycles through the rolling terrains around either of their family homes. But she hated the weekdays, when she was supposed to rise early to go to school at the Colegio de Santa Rita. She hated having to wear the ugly black shoes and the simply horrid uniforms. She found it tiresome to learn, among other things, literature, geometry and geography.

The Colegio de Santa Rita was a school for girls managed by Dominican nuns where all Arguelles girls have studied for the past one hundred years, from grade school until high school, as part of a family tradition. In Esperanza's opinion, she didn't need formal education in her life. She considered it too manly. She would have very much preferred to go to some sort of finishing school, which she read about in European magazines, in which she would be taught how to wear scarves, do her hair in the continental fashion, speak English with a Transatlantic accent, and finally get rid of her trilled r's. The last thing she needed in her life was geometry. The life she chose to lead now and would choose to lead in the future would not require that she know how to measure angles and planes and the distance from one point to another, and arcs and the inclines of lines and tetrahedrons. She felt that her life would not have more meaning if she encountered such things and knew how to deal with them. Indeed, there were lines and planes and cubes all over the house, but she did not build the house, and she had no plans to build one or even draw one on paper.

History, too, she didn't like. Long-dead people who once sparked revolutions and who ended up being immortalized in encyclopaedias and paper currencies did not interest her. Unlike Assumpta, who, at a very early age, strove to find connections between maps and their inks and the significance between and among them, Esperanza did not have the capacity to make these connections. These ancient people did not interest her, because she did not connect their achievements and sacrifices with the liberties she was now enjoying in her life.

For geography, she felt a complete indifference. If, and when, she would travel, it would be beside the man of her dreams. He would be a tall, handsome, dashing, wealthy man who would enhance her already-honourable stature in society. He would act as her sophisticated and learned tour guide when he would bring her to exotic countries and show her inside grand palaces and great museums and wonderful vistas or hills and oceans. He would introduce her to the most powerful men in international society and their wives. As far as she knew, to know geography—and history—was the job of this man, not hers.

Nor did she like literature. All of the books she was made to read were written by boorish American men. Philippine folk tales she found just too silly. In fact, there was little about her studies that she liked. She went through school grudgingly, dragging herself out of bed for it, fulfilling her homework nightly with much sighing; so much flapping and shuffling of papers, tearing up of drafts and filling of pens with inks several times. These were all to display her suffering as if she were already in some sort of purgatory.

But one thing she did love in school were her piano lessons and her voice lessons with Miss Hidalgo. Herself a rather short, middle-aged woman with a short temper and massive hips, Miss Hidalgo's appeal for Esperanza lay not so much on her physical beauty, or her ability to teach and her methodology of doing it. Instead, Esperanza's fascination with Miss Hidalgo was based on the rumours that Miss Hidalgo once had a long, tempestuous love affair with a handsome man from a great family, but he had to let go of her because he had to go into politics and marry another woman, whom his family chose for him. For this reason, Miss Hidalgo had never loved again, and instead, withdrew into the confines of her large, bright music room, singing heart-rending Italian sonatas in soprano and playing doleful Spanish love songs on the grand piano that was at the centre of the room.

So Esperanza didn't mind Miss Hidalgo whenever the teacher was being intractably stern, and dealt with her students as if they were troopers required to follow a specific formula. Her way of teaching piano was as if it were more of a science than an art.

'*Legato!*' Miss Hidalgo would burst out, her conductor's baton snapping the knuckles of Esperanza's guilty hand.

'*Mira!* From the beginning! Go!' Miss Hidalgo would say, standing beside Esperanza, her arms across her bosom.

Then snap the ruler would go again, hitting Esperanza's knuckles. 'Stop! I do not hear the trill! You have to trill this measure! The sign is right there! You are not blind! See that? *Otra vez!*'

'Your wrist is dropping!'

'Your knuckles are coming up again!'

'You are over-reaching for the flat key because your entire hand is on the wrong part. Place it higher up! *Alta! Alta!*'

These, Esperanza didn't mind. Since she liked Miss Hidalgo, she even paid attention to how she got mad and considered copying her expressions of anger when the opportunity arises.

What Esperanza looked most forward to at the end of the school day—before suffering histrionically through her homework—was the chance to chat with her friends on the telephone. It was mostly with Sofia, who was the one who whetted her appetite for the telephone to begin with, and over the telephone they would make fun of the people in school that they didn't like, and giggle over private jokes. When Luningning, their *majordoma*, or head housekeeper, would appear suddenly at the entrance to the living room and look pointedly at her, that was her cue that her telephone time was over. Then Esperanza would go to the den where everyone studied, to go through the daily melodramatic show of doing her homework. Only after dinner could Esperanza retire to her bedroom, her romance novels, her magazines, her examination of her eyebrows. After she has made sure that her eyebrows were still completely to her liking, she would lie in bed dreaming about the man she would marry and the countries they would travel to and the people they would meet, until she fell asleep.

Her father would be home from the farms at around eight o' clock every night, rest for about half an hour in his library, then join his family in for dinner. Often Jacobo went over the farms with Jacobo II, the first-born son, who was now fifteen and had been studying at the Holy Rosary Minor Seminary since he was thirteen. Jacobo II was not yet as quiet as his father; the constant companionship of his sister, the hyperactive, thin and wiry Inez who was just a year younger than him but already taller than him, and who secretly kept a *bolo* under her bed, helped influence him to voice out his thoughts most of the time. The two of them would usually spend time together outside in the fields, looking over the high points of the rolling hills in one of their farms, having lunch under a tree or by the banks of the irrigation, or just riding their horses through the plains. Jacobo II often imagined Inez to be the Athena of the mythology he had read from one of the books from Jacobo's library. He had also figured out early in his life that war, as well as the management of a large system of farms, suited Inez more than it did him.

When he wasn't with Inez, he was quieter, had less ideas, was less energetic, was more passive, and preferred to stay in his room or under a tree to read the classics. He preferred them over the theology lessons that were the staple at the *seminario*, teachings that he found altogether too dogmatic and at the same time full of contradictions. But the novels he read from his father's library kept him up at nights. It was whenever he dropped by his father's library every once in a while to return some books and to get new ones that he often ran into Assumpta. She would most likely be sitting on the floor, sometimes beside Mrs Palacio, her nanny, with open Atlases around her, the series of illustrated Dickens opened to the illustrations. He knew that she loved to go through the pictures and imagine worlds through them, just like she imagined worlds from the images of the maps she now keeps secret in her tender, fragile, seven-year-old heart. But most of the time, Jacobo II would find her in the library alone.

Once, coming upon her going through the pages of *A Christmas Carol*, Jacobo II asked her, 'What's your favourite book from here?'

'This one,' Assumpta piped up, her eyes wide and sparkling. 'The one with the ghosts. I love the ghosts!'

'Why do you love the ghosts? They are scary. Don't they scare you?' Jacobo II asked, sitting beside her on the floor.

'Of course not. I love ghosts! I think they know things we don't, and we can learn a lot if we just talk to them.'

'But you can't talk to ghosts.'

'Of course you can! Look at this picture,' she said, pointing to an illustration. 'The mean man is talking to the ghost, and then afterwards the man becomes a good person. He's no longer mean.'

Jacobo II paused for a while and gravely answered, 'I see what you mean.'

Assumpta smiled at him with her wide mouth and laughed.

'May I borrow the book when you're done with it?' Jacobo II asked.

'Sure! I'll leave it on the shelf for you,' she said, stretched her neck to kiss Jacobo II on the cheek, and promptly went back to flipping through the books. She slowly caressed the pages and ran her little fingers through the lines in the illustrations. She was completely engrossed in her bubble, which made the rest of the world disappear like one of her maps that had faded away, as if Jacobo II was no longer there. He left the library quietly, in deep thought, a few books under his arms.

On his way to his room, he passed by the small front room, where Guadalupe, the fourth child, now eleven, sat by the window working on her needlework. On the sofa beside her was their Abuelita, her grandmother, their father's mother, Mercedes Robles viuda de Arguelles, who had always worn purple since the day he first saw her. She was all of seventy-nine, but her eyesight was as sharp as an eagle's. She had taken Guadalupe under her wing, and was even the one who gave the girl her name, even when she was still in the womb, because Mercedes had predicted that Margarita was carrying a girl. She had already given up on Esperanza, who, as far as Mercedes was concerned, was too modern and was therefore Margarita's problem. Jacobo II was Jacobo's charge, Inez was incorrigible and manly and hopeless and could fend for herself as far as Mercedes cared. Both Paz and Assumpta were still too small and heedless for her to know, and thus she could not ponder over the possibilities of their respective destinies.

Guadalupe, on the other hand, Mercedes had quite high hopes for. Even as a child she could observe that Guadalupe had the propensity to be pious, quiet, submissive, yet at the same time displayed an amazing depth of perception and cunning that allowed her to get what she wanted by asking for them at the perfect time, in the perfect way. The effect often was that her benefactor gladly and quickly granted her the request while feeling pleased and smug, as if it was their idea to begin with. It was not quite the same strain of overt, piercing and sometimes operatic manipulative-ness that Arguelles women were known for but Mercedes could see how much more effective Guadalupe's style was. In that sense, Mercedes could see that of all of Jacobo's children, it was Guadalupe who had more wiles, hidden under her apparent piety, and thus had more choices in life open to her, and more power in her hands.

Guadalupe, in her quiet, introspective way, knew this as well. She was the most observant of all the Arguelles children, and throughout the years had almost perfected the art of being almost invisible in a room until people had forgotten she was still there. That is when they would talk about things she was not supposed to hear. Everything she heard she kept to herself as little sources of clout, little aces up her sleeve. In those moments, she learnt so much about the nature and characteristics of each member of the family and of some of their friends and visitors that she knew that someday she would be able to use that knowledge to her advantage to get what she wanted. Over time, even in her tender eleven years, her small, lacy, delicate sleeves had become full and heavy with these aces, most of them accidentally collected. She knew she had power, but did not yet know exactly how special this power was. But she did have an inkling that it was the kind of power that moved things into motion through other people, leaving Guadalupe herself spotless, innocent, and free to go through her life with impunity.

Thus, the Arguelles children were wildly different from each other in interests, intellect, personal choices, and world perspective. The only thing that tied them together, aside from their bloodline, was that they looked very much alike. Tall, solidly build yet a little bit fleshy, with the fair, fair skin of Margarita, and with the patrician nose and stern grey eyes of Jacobo. They all had an upright bearing and a special kind of studied walk and a careful way of speaking and conducting themselves in public. Mercedes started teaching all of them this bearing the moment each of them turned four years old, and they retained most of the training, except for Inez, who had the habit of throwing proper manners into the air whenever she was out in the fields alone. The children also did believe in many of the same things, like in family loyalty and respect for ancestry. What brought them most together, though—these six disparate children chained together by blood and destiny and the mystery of their origins—was their love for Camarines. They were raised by their parents to consider no other place as home, and that their house, built by the first Arguelles almost two hundred years ago, would stand forever to give them shelter and sanctuary. They grew up believing that the house would be their fortress for as long as Arguelleses continued to walk the lands of Camarines.

Chapter 2

The House at Hacienda Marianita

The house that sheltered such an abundance of varying priorities, passions and drives was itself also a sprawling affair, and bore witness to all of these for close to two centuries. Because so many Arguelleses had lived in the house for so long, many changes had been made to the house without much planning and consideration for the original intentions of the design. This turned the house into something of a monstrosity.

The house was built in 1784 by Sebastian Arguelles for his wife, Marianita Enojado, and named in her honour. But that was all anyone now knew about the house and the ancestors. Before the sudden arrival of the Arguelleses on Camarines soil, nothing was known, and the rest of the story had become an amalgamation of rumours and unfinished histories. The story of the house, however, was intact, continuing and deathless.

The house was a very large two-storey building that spanned over 1,800 square metres of land. It was three kilometres away from the only concrete public road that connected the many towns of Camarines together. The driveway to the house was wide and gravelled, banked by wide-canopied trees. A huge black wrought-iron gate loomed beneath the shadows, an ornate M worked into the bars. The gate was guarded by Rotillo, who had had that job since anyone could remember. Thin, stooped, and eternally dressed in black pants and a white shirt, he was childless, never married, and talked to no one except to those who wished to enter the premises of the house. He had a lackey whom he would order to run to the house in case a visitor came. When the lackey returned with orders to let the visitor in, Rotillo would pull a thick rope that would lift a heavy iron bar that locked the gate, and two other guards would pull the gates inwards to let the visitor in.

The driveway was flanked by even more shade trees. There were more guards here with bolos tied to their waists. They wove in and out through the trees, crossing the street randomly, sometimes talking among themselves, sometimes chewing tobacco while resting on hammocks hidden among the thickets behind the trees. Other guards were posted as sentinels all over the grounds of the house. Their head guard was Pato, who wielded a shotgun and a revolver.

After a slight bend, the facade of the house presented itself like a stern, elegant *doña*, or society lady. The first floor was made of stone and etched with lines and decorated with brass appliqués. Its large main doors were made of heavily carved wood. Leading up to those doors were a set of wide *señorita* steps made of stone, steps with risers that were only six inches tall. These were flanked on both sides by twin statues of women carrying a vat of water over their shoulders. The windows around the first floor were open but barred, while the balconies upstairs showed fluttering lace curtains and glimpses of decorated ceilings, grand chandeliers, and the tops of canopy beds.

The grounds surrounding the house were covered with blue grass, and the flower beds were laid on a grid, with stone walkways. The larger plants and shrubs were relegated to the perimeter of grounds, shrubbery that offered a hiding place for children during their games. Sometimes, Jacobo II would sit on the grounds to read, away from Inez, who, when she couldn't find him, would simply abandon her search and ride out into the fields all by herself.

The house also had a much smaller inner garden that was accessed from the double sliding doors of a large *lanai*, or a Spanish veranda. All these gardens were regularly tended by gardeners who had been working for the family for many years, and many of them were second- and third-generation gardeners, who had inherited their providence and their servitude from their forefathers. Many of the other servants in the house were also descendants of older ones. Such was the setup of the house's inner machinery—designations were inherited, skills were passed on, and lives that had expired were continued by others next in line. It was a very orderly setup. It was this well-oiled machinery that gave the house its sense of order. Luningning made sure that this was so.

The gardens were immaculate and symmetrical, the servants were capable and efficient, and the daily life of the entire house followed a productive routine. But the actual, physical house itself, that very structure in which everybody moved and lived, was by no means symmetrical or orderly. It certainly had a definite and orderly floor plan when first built. But over the decades, as the family grew, more space was needed inside, so more rooms were built, which necessitated additional hallways, stairs, steps, walls, all made to go around what was already there. Nothing was taken down; every new thing was an addition, never a replacement. So what began as a presumably neat, symmetrical, traditional Spanish house with wide windows and wraparound porches gradually evolved into a transmogrification of halls that led to the same rooms, corridors that led to nowhere or back to themselves, rooms located inside larger rooms, and rooms that no one knew the purpose of. Some rooms were completely sealed off, their windows boarded up, and no one seemed to have the keys to them. Some rooms had two doors, and some doors led back to the same rooms, and some of the closets had been plastered over. Some of the walls were not even real walls.

A part of the wraparound balcony on the second floor was also blocked off to give way to a small room, to be used for caging myna birds, but the birds died after only two weeks, although the servants never failed to care for them. The birds were never replaced. After a while, Margarita thought of placing an arboretum in the space to make use of the northern light, but the plants all died after two weeks. The gardener had to endure Margarita's admonitions for five days straight. Then Mercedes thought of placing a large aquarium of goldfish in the area, and all the fish also died after two weeks. Some of the servants began whispering that the portion was cursed, that no living thing could stay alive there beyond the second week.

Assumpta, on the other hand, could not care less about such curses. She went to that balcony once a week and stayed there making drawings of birds and trees and hills, and tacked them on to the screens, and even tried to draw a map of the house basing from what she observed from her many days of wandering around. As she went through the house and discovered more, she would draw the maps as fast she could envision them, and then she would pick up another piece of paper and draw another new map to connect with the previous one she made.

On one of her solo forays, she found at the middle landing of the main staircase a low, square panel that moved on a hinge. Beyond it was a narrow set of stairs that led down, with a door at the landing. The door was locked, but the doorknob jiggled when she tried it. After a while, the doorknob came off in her hands and the door creaked open. She walked in, unafraid, to find one new room in the house. It was very dark, but she found that the lights still worked when she reached up on tiptoe to turn on the toggle switch by the door. She saw that it was a large room, large for a small seven-year-old, and she was quite pleased with what she found. The one window it had was shut tight and its panes were blacked out, so the room was clean and free of dust.

The room was completely empty, save for a white ceramic claw-foot bathtub, which was right in the centre of the room. This perplexed Assumpta. She did not understand what the room was for, or how anyone could take a bath in here. It did not look like how the bathrooms she had seen were usually built. Here the floor and walls were made of smooth unpainted concrete, but there was nothing inside other than the bathtub that would even hint that the room was, or used to be, a bathroom. There were no sinks, no visible plumbing, no toilet seat, not even a floor drain.

She went to the window and stood on tiptoe to open it. The pane swivelled outward with some creaking noises, and the fresh summer air came in. The window, unscreened, looked out on to the stables about half a kilometre away, and so Assumpta, with her keen sense of direction, thought that she must be somewhere near the servants' quarters and the kitchen.

It was a strange room, but Assumpta felt an instant liking for it. The feet of the bathtub looked like the claws of a dragon gripping a silver ball, and Assumpta found it adorable. The room as a whole appealed to her, and she noticed that it was a perfect square. It was probably the only perfectly square area that she had seen in the house.

The bedrooms, on the other hand, although open and breezy and comfortable, were confusing in their layout, like that of the rest of the house. They were like mazes with compartments and routes that doubled back into themselves, and more than one door that led out to the same passageway. There were a lot of strange corners of varying angles that suggested that something was behind them.

Assumpta and Paz shared the same bedroom, but their bedroom was located right inside Guadalupe's larger bedroom, with the large windows that she needed for doing her needlework. The inner bedroom had only one external wall and window. Guadalupe had a small bathroom inside her bedroom, which she shared with her two youngest sisters. Guadalupe's room led out to a corridor across from a much smaller room occupied by Mrs Palacio. Before the nanny could tuck both of the smallest children into bed, she had to enter Guadalupe's bedroom, pass by her bed already neatly turned down, and go through the door to the smaller room. To go back to her own room she had to go back the same way. For this reason, no one locked their bedroom doors, giving the false impression that no one in the house had secrets to hide.

But they did. Everyone in the house had, secrets of different kinds. Assumpta had her own secrets about the significance of the fading maps and fading worlds in her father's library. Guadalupe had her secret cunning, while Esperanza had her secret dreams of being powerful and famous in a faraway place, with a rich and powerful husband. Inez was empowered by her secret bolo and her secret defiance at having to conform to how her family believed she should act, be, and live, and that because she was a girl, decisions must be made for her and not by her. Jacobo II had this secret dislike for his future of being the next manager of the *hacienda*, which is what the entire farm holdings of the Arguelleses was called. Jacobo lived with his secret relief at not having to bed Margarita for the remaining years of his life, while Margarita kept secret her falling out of love with Jacobo. Mercedes, in her antiquity, was kept alive by the secret knowledge of what had gone on in the house many years before. Only Paz, it seemed, had no secrets.

Mercedes Robles viuda de Arguelles, who did not carry a drop of Arguelles blood in her veins, had lived in the family and carried its name for so long that she might as well be a true-blooded one. She had been promised to Alfonso Arguelles since she was fourteen, as part of a pact between her family and Alfonso's, and they were married when she was seventeen. She left behind the traditions and systems of the Robleses of Cavite, travelled to Camarines, and lived out the rest of her life as best as she could as an Arguelles. She took this mission into her heart and soul out of respect for her husband and the family they would be building together.

She was terrified, of course. Only seventeen years old and uprooted from the house she was born in, she felt like a straw floating in a vast ocean. The first step she took beside Alfonso into the front doors of the house suddenly made her feel cold, as if there was a warning in the air, hinting that she should not be complacent in the house. The foyer was large, breezy from the open front doors, cool from the tiled floor, the light from the outside reflected into a multitude of slivers by the small chandelier overhead. The foyer opened out to the front sala, the wide staircase, and the arched great doors of the ballroom beyond. Nothing looked ominous and dark in the foyer, but it felt like something was being placed ever so gently on her shoulders.

She did not feel unwelcome; she just felt that the house was trying to make her aware of something. '*Cuidado*,' a wisp of wind whispered into her ear. 'Be careful.' She stopped for a second, looked around the cool, bright, welcoming foyer warily. Alfonso took her hand gently and led her forward into the main hallway, and the ominous feeling slowly went away. Such was the house's welcome for Mercedes. It was also how all other Arguelles wives were received the moment they stepped into the house.

The house itself had its own secrets. Most houses do, especially very old houses, but this one was different. Its history was filled with malice, deception, destruction, thefts of massive proportions. Its walls had been witness to pacts made to completely ruin the family's enemies and the enemies of its allies. Its tables and desks were platforms upon which these plots were made and finalized. Through its doorways, people ran through to report on the success or the failure of the plots laid. The house had not been mere witness to terrible, syndicated, organized crimes. The house itself has been an accomplice, by providing shelter and seclusion to the evil that unfolded for much of two hundred years.

If there was ever a map of the house as it stood now, it would no longer be the same as the map of the house that Sebastian Arguelles had built for Marianita Enojado. After Marianita slipped in the bathroom and hit her head hard on the corner of the sink and subsequently died of head trauma, Sebastian kept more and more to himself. He focused only on how to acquire more land for the hacienda, as if trying to fill the void created by Marianita's death, by making the hacienda as powerful and as vast as he could. He gradually lost touch with his own children, ceased to tell them his plans for their future, stopped telling them stories, no longer shared with them bits and pieces of the family history. He became the catalyst for plunging the house into an asylum for words unsaid, feelings unexpressed, and relationships left behind to fade.

As part of his plan to make the hacienda bigger, he also made the house bigger. He added rooms inside rooms, added an additional floor to a part of the western section of the house, expanded the kitchen to be able to feed the growing number of workers for the growing expanse of land he kept acquiring, all the while closing up the rooms that Marianita frequented.

He had her bedroom sealed off, the water pipes to her bathroom cut off, the windows boarded up. And then he had two more locks added to the door. Where the keys to these rooms were now, no one knew.

Sebastian also had the smaller living room at the back part of the house sealed off. That was where Marianita used to do her needlework and her reading, her eyes favouring the mid-afternoon sun after siesta. That was where she wrote letters to her family and relatives abroad, and that was where she took the catnaps that she loved. On top of this part of the house, he had a third floor built, where he began to take office as soon as it was finished. That was where he trained Enrique and Amadeo, his two eldest sons, to manage the hacienda. Then he built another floor on top of that, which was just as large as his third-floor office, to which only he had access. This created a tower-like structure that rose from the western part of the house that, against the setting sun, looked like a lonely, emaciated watchman. No one knew what was in that fourth-floor bedroom and no one knew what he did there, it after he died. He had always kept that bedroom locked when he had to leave it. No one ever found the keys to that bedroom even after he was found dead inside his third-floor office one morning by the maid who brought him his coffee, despite the ardent efforts of two sons to find them. He was ninety-seven years old. Until his very last day, he had worked for the glory of the hacienda, under the shadow of his sorrow and his longing for the wife he had lost about half a century before.

Those were the configurations of the house as Sebastian left it to his heirs. Over time, the house was further transformed by Arguelleses that followed, to suit needs, whims, architectural fads, superstitions. Maps of these various evolutions of the house had long been lost. The family was not very keen on keeping records of something that they woke up to every morning and slept in every night, so the many changes to the house remained undocumented and unexplained.

But the house remembered its transformation. It remembered every single nail driven into its walls over the years, every dovetail, every panel of wood, every pane of glass, every piece of furniture and fixture that was brought in. It remembered every word said within its walls, including those whispered in confidence. The house was alive and its memory was vivid and immense, and its secrets were carried in the immensity of its foundations and the confused manner of its layout. The people in the house may have had their own little, mortal, finite secrets, but the house was older, and carried more burden than any individual Arguelles ever could.

The house's secrets were deep and venomous, but it had not always been a host to evil. It still remembered the times before all the clashes for power happened. The house had known love and integrity and friendship, and honour. But the Arguelles blood that gave the house its foundations and its life was rich with a hunger for power, thus the warning the house gave to every non-Arguelles-blooded wife when she first walked in through the main doors of the house.

The house was made with the intention of raising a happy family in it, and subsequent generations of happy and well-rounded Arguelles descendants, naturalized Filipinos, who would love Camarines as their own. But in time, as part of its destiny, the once-happy house had been made to witness corruption, and had been thus corrupted against its will. Guilt ran through its corridors, wafted through its windows, pervaded its rooms that were occupied by the generations still living. It dwelled in the sealed-off rooms, in the plastered-up walls, in the dank passageways that lay snaking through the underbelly of the house like a giant serpent. Indeed, the house's guilt had grown powerful and alive.

The enormous tension of such guilt could not help but try to find some form of release by allowing the guilt to manifest in certain forms. Thus, every once in a while, strange beings walked the maze-like corridors of the house, making themselves heard, laughing, whispering, tapping the walls, leaving behind cold drafts, faint hand prints on walls, wet oily footprints of bare feet on the polished parquet floors, and trails of aromas of flowers and candles. The servants had no lack of possible explanations for these; most of their hushed stories expectedly bordering on the occult, mentioning names popular in ancient Philippine folklore—*kapre, manananaggal, tiyanak, tikbalang, nuno sa punso, wak-wak*—alive long before the Spanish came into these pagan islands. But the beings in the house of the Arguelleses came not from Philippine folklore, but oozed forth from family guilt.

Mercedes was not unsympathetic to these beings of the house. Since the moment she first walked into the house with Alfonso she knew they were there, and had been there for a long time. Eventually, she realized that the house was warning her, a non-Arguelles by blood, that she herself would not be culpable, but her new name and the fresh Arguelles bloodline she would give life to would drag her down together with the real-blooded ones.

So she kept to herself, striving to refrain from speculation. She focused on her wifely duties. She obeyed Alfonso's every instruction and catered to his every need, making it her mission in life to serve him. She considered herself a part of a greater plan over which she had no control. She felt herself powerless over such things as destiny, the Robles women not being quite as aggressive and old a family as the Arguelleses. Maybe, she thought, being from a younger family that had been beset by fewer struggles over the years, she was not required to deal with more than what she was capable of.

She considered this a blessing, and held on to this thought secretly, which gave her the stomach to be an Arguelles for the rest of her life.

Assumpta, the youngest in the family, was still unburdened by the savagery that Mercedes felt was her duty to harbour in her own shrivelled, non-Arguelles heart. The unfettered Assumpta was the only one who could make Jacobo smile. She was his favourite and the only one given free rein in the house, when all the others were prohibited from visiting certain areas and rooms in it.

When Assumpta was much younger, Margarita had ordered Mrs Palacio to follow her everywhere, but Mrs Palacio, then being already sixty, could not keep up with the child's constant running and hiding and going into dark and dusty places. So Mrs Palacio gave up, and informed Margarita, who just shrugged her shoulders, for she herself knew how hyperactive Assumpta was. So the girl was left pretty much alone most of the time, her life requiring her only two hours to sit still in the classroom to practice her writing and her reading and lectures of catechism, for five days a week.

Since she was young enough to create and indulge in her own fantasies, the hushed tales regarding the history of the Arguelleses and the house failed to affect her. Instead, she dreamed up different worlds, worlds far away from the Arguelles house, far away from the present time, worlds that came into being once maps of them were drawn, and disappeared when the inks on the maps disappeared over time. For Assumpta, land lived only as long as the ink was decipherable on the paper that showed its map.

Of course she wondered about the house, which she simply adored, and believed that somewhere within such a wondrously crooked house, there must be a map of it. Surely someone at some point of time, must have needed a map in order not to get lost inside, and she decided that she must find this map.

She wanted to know where Marianita's room was. She wanted to go inside Sebastian's bedroom on the top floor of the house. She wanted to know how Mercedes's maid was able to come up to her room to bring her breakfast in bed every morning at six o'clock, without passing through any of the hallways from the kitchen that she could see. Surely there were other passageways and rooms in this fascinating beast of a house, and Assumpta wanted to know every single one, walk through them all, view the house from inside every single window, and lay claim to this enormous, bewildering space that gave her such a sense of wonder and happiness, and a strange sense of security.

She believed that such a map existed, because the house and those who lived there were still alive and breathing and working and eating and studying catechism and cursive handwriting. The map must still have its lines and labels clearly printed on the paper. She wanted to know the house, and she wanted the house to know her. Another reason she wanted to find the map was that she wanted to see just how clear the ink on the paper was. Were they a house and a family that was on the verge of disappearing into nothingness? Or would the ink be indelible and thus ensure the existence of the Arguelles family forever? And if she did find a map and the ink on it was already fading, could she trace over the fading lines to save the existence of her house and her family for much longer? Those were the thoughts that constantly roiled in her mind and disturbed her to no end. But she could not tell anyone this, as she swore to herself to keep her map theory a secret on the night of the storm, when Paz told her she was crazy. Yet, the more that Assumpta kept this a secret, the more she believed in her heart that there was such a map and that she would find it. So she began with her mission.

Assumpta started with Mercedes. One afternoon, after her school work, she joined Mercedes and Paz in the dining room for *merienda*, the local afternoon repast. They had sandwiches, biscuits and traditional Spanish chocolate. Paz, always a fast eater, finished hers and then ran off outside.

'Abuelita,' Assumpta began timidly. 'Is there a map of the house?'

Mercedes chuckled, '*Hija, querida.*' These were her usual terms of endearment. 'This house has been changed so much over the years that whatever map there once used to be would be useless.'

'But wouldn't people need a map to not get lost in the house?'

'Well, that's true,' Mercedes replied, looking thoughtful. 'But we have all been here so long that we never needed one.'

'How about the servants? Don't they get lost inside without a map?'

'Oh no. They almost never leave the kitchen. And the dining room is directly upstairs from the kitchen,' Mercedes chuckled again. 'No one needs a map for that.'

Assumpta nodded thoughtfully, finished her milk, and decided to go a different route on another day.

Next, she tried Mrs Palacio. One afternoon, in the schoolhouse with Paz, she did her handwriting exercises really well, and Mrs Palacio appeared pleased.

Almost immediately after Paz ran off to the dining room to have her milk and merienda, Assumpta asked her, 'Mrs Palacio, does this house have a map?'

'This house?' Her already wrinkled brow wrinkled even more. 'I don't know, *chica*. I came here only about twenty years ago.'

'But how do you get to where you need to go? Don't you get lost?'

'I only go to my bedroom, your bedroom, the kitchen, and the schoolroom. I don't need to know much of the house. It tires me to walk around so much.' She sighed, sat down and twirled her ankles with her feet still in her low-heeled shoes. 'I am too old.'

'No, you're not. Abuelita is much older than you and she still walks around the house a lot.'

'She owns this house,' Mrs Palacio sighed again. 'She should walk around in it.'

'But Papa also owns the house, and he doesn't go around in it as much as Abuelita does.'

'Don Jacobo is the man of the hacienda, and his job is in the fields. The house is always left to the ladies of the house. Men cannot be bothered by matters such as housekeeping.'

'Why doesn't Mama go around so often then? She is a lady of the house.'

Mrs Palacio sighed again, and straightened her back. 'Your mother has her own way of seeing that the house is functioning well. We have Luningning who oversees everything. Besides, Doña Margarita has her preoccupations.'

Margarita's current preoccupation was Esperanza's eighteenth birthday, which was the age at which girls were given their formal debut into society, and it was usually a major occasion for the family and a major social event for their circle. Margarita was the one who came up with the guest list, sent out the invitations, and tracked the RSVP replies. She was the one who hand-picked the dressmakers and the dress designs. She was the one who decided to have the event held inside the Arguelles house, and in preparing the house for the big-name guests who would arrive, she had hired extra help to completely clean the large ballroom. Drapes have been ordered and couches have been reupholstered. The old rugs have been replaced with newer ones. Some of the storage rooms were opened and out emerged the decorative family heirlooms, mirrors, portraits, silverware, china, candlesticks and others.

So, for the next several weeks, the house was in a state of tense anticipation. Every day, buckets of water and long brooms were brought into the ballroom, which had been closed for more than a decade, to clear out the dust that had already encrusted the floors and walls and windows. Crumbling clusters of wallpapers were peeled off, and the walls were painted a very pale salmon pink. The giant chandeliers have been brought down to be polished, checked, rewired and then hung up again. The frescoes and mouldings on the ceiling were painstakingly scrubbed with soap and water to reveal the whiteness underneath the years of dust and grime and neglect. That proved how long the Arguelleses had not hosted any major social event. It was always the Monsantillo family, who lived in the next town, that took the initiative to host soirees. But because of Esperanza, this dry social spell would be broken.

Esperanza imagined this to be an event to remember for decades to come. However, all these were not only for Esperanza, but also for the centuries-old tradition that the Arguelleses had followed. This tradition needed to be witnessed by all the other powerful families who, together with the Arguelleses, had given their names to much of the portions of land of Camarines.

Chapter 3

Blood Ties

Camarines was a very large province in the region of the Philippines called Bicol. It was located somewhere between almost the southern end of the island of Luzon and its very centre. Camarines was accessible by a single concrete road that began in Manila and stretched for about 400 kilometres to reach Camarines, and stretched further beyond. Camarines itself was a sprawling space, hilly and dry in some parts, flat and swampy in others. It had its share of forests, lakes, beaches, waterfalls, mountains and plantations. It was an obese and fecund giant that heaved and breathed in time with the wet and dry seasons, regularly bringing forth a profusion of greenery from its dark, mossy, humongous womb.

To anyone travelling through, unfamiliar with Camarines, the place was marked with what looked like large tracts of unused and seemingly unowned land. But according to the maps of Camarines, every single speck of land has been legally owned for almost two hundred years by only three different families: the Visbal, the Monsantillo and the oldest of them all, the very first ones to step foot in Camarines, the Arguelles. On paper, no one else had rights to the yields and the legacies of the land of Camarines but these three families.

If a genealogy tree of these three families would be drawn, from the time Sebastian Arguelles and Marianita Enojado arrived in Camarines and began their bloodline, each family's tree would eventually grow into what would look like a raging baobab with tangled branches all over its trunk. Its Herculean roots would reach down towards the very bowels of the earth, and then through to the lush under-terrain of Spain from where it leeched its ancestral traditions and its most essential qualities that kept it alive in Camarines. Its canopies would span many square kilometres of earth, its branches twisting and intertwining with each other. From that would further sprout even more twigs and shoots and other branches that would snake up and out of the giant, convoluted canopy of a genealogy that had practically lived and died and lived again, continuously. Each mammoth baobab that stood for each family, although inextricably interconnected, nevertheless sustained itself only by the merit of one common and inescapable gene of doom.

Surely, of families this old and this enmeshed with each other, there should be an actual written genealogy. It should be maintained and constantly updated by commissioned scholars, hidden in a library somewhere in one of the houses of the three haciendas that controlled the lands of Camarines. But if such a genealogy existed, it has never been found, and the truth is that no such record of genealogy had ever existed. Because these families believed that nothing in their lifeline would ever change throughout the centuries that would come, and if no change is to happen, no records were needed. What was, is also what is, and shall continue eternally. They find their security in tradition and in preserving their lifeblood via the purity of their ancient hereditary alliances. They assumed that children would always know who their parents were, and great-grandparents would always hand down an arsenal of jewellery, old letters, old agreements, old maps, and old portraits that would be sufficient to connect the present generation to the very beginning of its bloodline.

Such a characteristic, that of taking the past and the future for granted, was unique to the descendants of the three families. This shall prove to be the most powerful catalyst of their undoing. That was one of the portents that the Arguelles house moaned about in the night, in the dark and winding corridors, in the empty and dusty rooms that foreshadowed a future of decay and ruin. Aside from the house's knowledge of the abominations of the past, it also knew the house's future. That was why every new Arguelles wife was warned of something ominous, a message of unease, a hint that she must be careful. It was not up to her to do something; she herself would be incorrupt, but she must protect herself. The true-blooded Arguelles women were invulnerable to these warnings, largely because the thresholds of the houses they crossed as new wives were no longer that of the house at Hacienda Marianita but the houses of their husbands. But all Arguelles women that were not born so and who entered the house at Hacienda Marianita throughout the centuries were united in receiving this vague dreamlike premonition that stayed with them for the rest of their lives.

Esperanza was an Arguelles not only by blood but also by the full power of her impulsive temperament. She was wrapped up in all the wonderful, varicoloured, intoxicating whirls and eddies that surrounded the preparation to her formal introduction into society. She was both blind and deaf to everything else except each and every detail of her debut event, down to every single minute detail. She was constantly bickering with her mother about seed pearls and diamonds and rubies and heeled slippers made of glass, because at some point she wanted to be Cinderella. That was only until Margarita pointed out that if she wanted to be Cinderella, then the soirée would have to end at exactly midnight, so Esperanza quickly called off the idea.

They squabbled about flowers and where to place the lamps in the ballroom, they wrangled about gossamer and of rouge and of how to put up her long, waist-length hair.

'Mama, I want to wear Doña Esmeralda's tiara.' Esmeralda Visbal was the wife of Enrique Arguelles, and she walked down the aisle to become an Arguelles while bearing on her proud head the tiara currently being discussed.

'It would not be proper to wear a tiara if you prefer to wear your hair down.'

'Then I'll have my hair in a *chignon* so I can wear the tiara.'

'If you wear your hair in a chignon and wear the tiara, we have to change the neckline of your gown. And then you cannot wear the diamond choker if you are already wearing a tiara. That's too much jewellery. It would look like you're trying too hard. Like someone not used to owning jewellery.'

'Really, Mama! What use are they if we can't use them?'

'Oh, we can use them, indeed,' Margarita said, an eyebrow raised. 'Just not all of them at once. You would look more like a Christmas tree than a debutante. Is that what you want? What would the Visbales whisper about you?'

'I am not saying that I want to wear all of them at once!' Esperanza shrieked, and threw herself onto her bed, her face all scrunched up.

Margarita left the room, shaking her head, longing for the day when it would all be over and also dreading the day when her three other daughters would be going through the same wretchedness with her, in their own time. It quickly flitted through her mind that Inez might not be so much trouble there.

Esperanza sulked, and then rose to go to the living room to call Sofia Monsantillo. What followed was a rather tearful discussion regarding the neckline of her gown, the choker, and the profound and world-changing issue of Esmeralda's tiara, and how cruel Margarita can be.

Mercedes kept herself out of the range of battle, simply waiting for the time when the both of them had decided on a truce. Mercedes decided that only when that happens will she go to the bank, extract the requisite pieces of jewellery from the safety deposit box, and then deposit them back there on the morning after the event.

Mercedes, of course, knew exactly why Esperanza and Margarita treated the event as something of great import, because she knew just how judgemental the two other families could be. The Visbales especially were a particularly scathing breed. Only one Visbal, the Esmeralda of the tiara that Esperanza and Margarita had been quarrelling about, ended up marrying an Arguelles. The rest of the Visbales decided to marry mostly their own third cousins and fourth cousins from then on, resulting in a peculiar line of people named Visbal-Visbal, and Visbal viuda de Visbal, who were often characterized by their long and thin countenance and bad, yellow, European teeth. They were able to retain their light-green eyes, their aquiline noses, and their blond hair, but they were also prone to a host of ailments and maladies. Cataracts, nearsightedness, migraine attacks, skin asthmas, gout, diabetes, arthritis, heart diseases, hypertension—it was an endless list. They shunned any form of activity that involved being directly under the sun, causing them to be very light-skinned, almost transparent.

The people of Camarines still talked about Juana Visbal, the youngest daughter of Alvaro Visbal and his third cousin Teresa. She was born in 1875 and was normal as a child. She had the usual Visbal features of aquilineness and paleness and quietude. However, when she turned twelve, she began to grow blind, and the blinder she got, the noisier she became. She would walk the halls of the house at Hacienda Dolores at all hours, ranting loudly.

'Rats! Snakes!' These were the words the Visbales would often wake up to in the middle of the night.

'I am cold!' she would also say.

A servant would come running with a shawl, but Juana would fling her arm out against the garment being proffered.

'Hot! It's hot!' She would then call out. The servants never knew what to do. Many of them would leave the Visbal household in quick succession.

Teresa would then come, take Juana's hand, and gently lead her back to her bedroom, which had nothing but a bedframe and mattress. All other furniture that had once been there had been taken out because Juana would try to get inside the drawers and the shelves in the closets, constantly wounding and bruising herself in the process.

'I must hide!' She would shout. 'Big rat!'

Juana was a small girl, and she actually did fit inside one of the compartments of her closet, and while she was inside she was uncharacteristically quiet. So for hours the entire household almost went crazy looking for her.

Sometimes she would find her way to the kitchen to eat raw meat, despite her blindness. The servants screamed and fled when they saw her chewing on a piece of tendon that was supposed to be cooked for lunch. It was such a grotesque sight. Later on the servants would whisper and speculate among themselves, venturing their own analyses regarding the reasons for Juana's strange behaviour.

'The Señorita smelt her way to the kitchen.'

'She could smell meat from far away. Like a predator. Her sense of smell became stronger when she became blind.'

'The Señorita is probably possessed by the devil.'

'That can be the only reason why she keeps shouting about rats and snakes.'

In the weeks that Juana was strangely ill, the Visbal household was in various levels of being understaffed, as servants left and were replaced, and then more would leave and be replaced, in an exhausting cycle that was bound in fear and confusion. Their majordoma, Marikit, suffered a mild stroke because of the stress, and the routines of the house fell in disarray. Mounds of laundry went unwashed, meals were cooked late and incorrectly, floors remained unswept, the dead flowers in the vases progressing into rot. The servants would randomly burst into tears while doing their tasks, and none of them would go near Juana's bedroom or ever be alone in the kitchen.

Alvaro and Teresa brought in an assortment of whatever doctors they could call from Manila, and who were willing to travel the long, long way to Camarines, but no cure was found. Teresa was at her wits' end. The whole house had been suffering for weeks. But she refused to accept the possibility that Juana was possessed.

'That is ridiculous!' she declared. 'My daughter has never even been outside. How could she have invited the devil inside of her?'

Juana's condition worsened quickly. She refused to be bathed or touched. But when she was alone in her room, she would take off all her clothes.

'Rain!' she would shout while disrobing. 'Raining snakes!'

One day, Teresa walked in while Juana was naked and saw that her daughter's skin had turned green and thick, and there was something that looked like moss growing in patches all over her torso and thighs. She screamed, and some of the servants came running. In a panic, someone decided it was best to take Juana outside into the sun right away.

She was quickly carried out into the garden, ranting and flailing, wrapped in a bed sheet, by seven servants. Once outside, they let her go. Teresa was there, by the doorway, staying out of the sun while crying almost hysterically and wringing her hands raw. Juana, right under sunlight, threw off the bed sheet. Her skin began to smoulder. The tips of the mossy green growth on her body glowed like tiny embers and grew into very small fires. Then her light-green eyes and light-coloured hair turned dark. She let out a scream and fell to the ground.

Her body started to emit more and more smoke, and no one could move. They all just stood there, transfixed, staring at the spectacle happening right in front of them in broad daylight. After several minutes, the body started to hiss, and then it combusted with a soft sound. Nothing was left of Juana except ashes.

For what seemed a very long time, no one moved or said a word. Then eventually, Pitong, the head gardener, felt it was his obligation to do something, as the garden was his jurisdiction and responsibility, so he took a bicycle and rode to the fields to tell Alvaro what happened. At first, Alvaro could not understand.

'Don Alvaro, I'm sorry. Señorita Juana is burnt,' Pitong, said. He was hunched over in front of Alvaro, unable to look at the Don directly.

'Burnt? What do you mean? She burnt herself? Was she playing with a match?' Alvaro asked loudly, feeling indignant.

'No, Don Alvaro. S-she herself became smoke and then t-turned into fire.' Pitong stammered while looking intently at Alvaro's knees, but tried to be as clear as he could, not wanting to be made to say that frightful statement all over again.

'She turned into fire,' Alvaro repeated, looking closely at Pitong.

'Don Alvaro, Señorita Juana is no more.' Pitong bowed his head even lower, now staring at Alvaro's boots. 'She is ashes.'

'I don't understand what you're saying, you old fool,' said Alvaro, very annoyed. 'I am going home.'

When Alvaro did get home, the other gardeners met him outside of the house and told him what had happened. He realized Pitong was not lying. Juana's ashes were right there. Alvaro stared at it for what seemed like hours, his body tensing up every second that his mind remembered all the details of Juana's condition that the house had had to endure. He remembered her small face and slight body wrapped in expensive clothes that seemed like rags on her because she was acting all mad and wretched.

Then he finally turned to the gardeners who had been standing behind him the whole time, silent and fearful.

'Gather the ashes. Place them in a pot, or a vase, or whatever receptacle you can find,' he said, and then walked towards the house. As he walked, he imagined Juana turning into fire, as Pitong had said, and then into ashes, and convinced himself that she was free, and that was what gave him relief, but he tried very hard not to reveal this relief that his daughter was finally dead.

Teresa was catatonic for months afterwards, and the servants who had witnessed what happened left the Visbal house and went back to their own families, sworn to secrecy and paid handsomely for their silence by Alvaro. Alvaro also took care of everything else. He had a casket purchased, and had a closed-casket wake for Juana, saying to anyone who asked that it would be hurtful for anyone to see the dead face of a twelve-year-old girl.

Of course in a town as small as theirs, even when the actual witnesses have sworn not to talk, such a bizarre account is bound to spread, although not at once, and not completely. Small details would be shared here and there, and questions asked about those details, which could only be answered with mere speculation. Over time, the story changed as it was passed on. The family did not keep documents, but Juana's death began their veering away from marrying their distant cousins.

The Visbales were the family that had the least number of members, because of the many miscarriages most likely caused by the long-term in-breeding. This was also probably the reason they were the most pious of the three powerful families of Camarines. They were quiet, soporific, melancholic and dour, though not quite reclusive. They did socialize with the other families every once in a while, and attended some political soirées that they were invited to. But they remained the family with the least drive, the weakest spirit, and the most uninterested in power and social connections. However, they were also the most fervent purveyors of the importance of family tradition and destiny.

The Monsantillos, though, the Arguelleses found almost at par with their own core values and traditions. The two families were joined together by virtue of a marriage between family members several generations back. That had started a long and productive alliance, which continued over time not by personal preference but by tradition. It was the Arguelleses that helped pave the way for the Monsantillos to have safe passage to Camarines. With all the politicking going on in Intramuros, the capital of Las Islas Filipinas in the late 1700s, the family's engineering of this migration that greatly benefitted them economically was no small feat.

Shortly after arriving in Camarines, the Monsantillos acquired their share of land in the province, in the town of Mangkono, and named it Hacienda Vida, in honour of the wife of Jaimito Monsantillo, who died before they left Spain. Jaimito was left with eight children ranging from the ages of four to sixteen. Jaimito's unmarried sisters, Emiliana and Conchita, took over the task of managing the household and the children. These sisters travelled with Jaimito and the children to Camarines.

The trip itself was long and arduous, but the Monsantillos were accommodated in one of the more luxurious galleons and had connections with the captain. They travelled in relative comfort, and the children did not suffer much.

As soon as the house was ready, Emiliana and Conchita set it up, employed servants and staff, made the arrangements for the schooling of the children, and mostly went on with their lives with as much patience and diligence as they could. Even after many years, in their hearts, they still mourned the death of their sister-in-law Vida, in a kind of mourning that is understated and secret, yet stays forever. Emiliana became the majordoma and Conchita became the children's nanny, and in this way the Monsantillos survived Vida's death.

The very first marriage that occurred within these families on Camarines soil was when Sebastian and Marianita's youngest daughter, Amparo, married Narciso Monsantillo, who was Jaimito and Vida's third-born son, in 1804. By virtue of that marriage, Amparo had become a Monsantillo and lived in the Monsantillo house until the very last of her days. Nothing was known about her happiness. No one kept records, and no one was left alive to remember.

Sebastian helped Jaimito design the Monsantillo house and have it built. It was a very large house, which was quite expected, even required. But unlike the Arguelles house, this one had rooms that were of the exact same size and layout, and all of their drapes matched all throughout the entire house. One week everything was a pale blue. The next week, everything was yellow. Next there could be white lace and doilies everywhere, or there could be red roses on every surface that could be found, including the bathrooms, according to the whims of the people that lived in the house.

The interior of the house was beautiful, orderly and well-planned. There were large rooms with right-angled corners and wonderfully appropriate dimensions. The windows were very large and almost always open to the breeze that came in from the hacienda's rolling small hills, in the distance. The main staircase was graciously wide and winding, with newel posts carved with an assortment of flowers and vines. The house was a pleasantly proportioned rectangle, its longer sides facing west and east, thereby getting the most light in both the morning and the afternoon. As one entered the main door, one could see the lanai doors in the near distance and the inner courtyard beyond it. The courtyard had beautiful, lush arbours, inviting and warm, promising quiet afternoons with friends and loved ones. The Monsantillo house rarely changed structurally, and Emiliana was good at keeping it in good shape during her time. The task of keeping the house in the exact same form was passed on to the succeeding Monsantillos, who were true to their mission. The house itself did not evolve, but the people living in it did. Eventually, people lost the memory of how the lands of Hacienda Vida were acquired, and the house, the only remaining witness to what had happened, seemed to be quiet about it in the meantime.

Over the years, the Monsantillo house seemed to have outgrown its sad origin. Now, the living room was often abuzz with the children of Salvador Monsantillo and Consuela Cabello playing songs they made up on the upright piano. It was bought for Marta, their second daughter and third-born, so she could practise playing her pieces every afternoon when she came home from school. Marta went to Colegio de Santa Rita, just like her older sister Sofia and Esperanza Arguelles, but was two years younger than them. When Marta wasn't using the piano, the youngest children, Heriberto who was nine and Beatriz who was six, were all over the piano, creating a tremendous ruckus in the living room.

They also pestered their nannies to no end by hiding behind curtains, under beds, and behind beside lamps, pretending to be ghosts that jumped out and cried, 'Boo!'. There were toys all over, and there were servants tasked just to pick up after the children for the entire day.

Beatriz was most inquisitive.

'Why is your name Bituin?' she asked one of the servants.

'Because when I was born, there was one star shining so brightly in the sky,' Bituin replied, scooping up a long wooden train from the floor.

'I don't believe you. There are no stars in the sky when it's day.'

'I was born at night,'

'How do you know that? You were a baby.'

'My mother told me.'

'What is your mother's name?'

'Ligaya,' Bituin sighed, and went down on all fours to fish out more toys from under the sofa.

'Why was she named that?'

'Why do you need to know?' an exasperated Bituin asked, upright but on her knees, with her hands on her hips, looking at Beatriz straight in the eyes because they were now of the same height.

'Because the lady that goes into my room at night says that I must give her names and their stories so she can make a very large quilt of names.' Beatriz widened her eyes and stretched her arms out to emphasize the largeness of the quilt that was to be made.

'What lady?' Bituin asks suddenly, staring with big eyes straight at Beatriz.

'The lady that makes the quilt.'

'Doña Corazon?' Bituin asked warily.

'Not Abuelita,' said Beatriz. Doña Corazon was Salvador's mother, and Beatriz had seen her portrait before. She pursed her lips, stood quietly in thought for a moment, then added, 'The quilt lady is younger. Like Mama.' She walked to the couch, climbed up, and sat on the top of the backrest. 'And she is always wearing blue.'

Bituin felt something rise up her back, and she shuddered. She had seen this lady, too, often from the corners of her eyes while going about her day. However, the lady was not fearsome to Bituin. She seemed lost, and often stood by the window of any room. She was calm but sad, and looked a lot like Beatriz. After the first few times, Bituin had wondered secretly about this lady in blue, never telling anyone, but after a while, the lady has become such a familiar albeit uncanny sight to her that she just took her for granted and assumed that only she could see her. It was thus a surprise to her to know that Beatriz could see her as well, and she found some relief that Beatriz did not seem afraid of the lady in blue. The rest of the house at Hacienda Vida, unknowing of the lady in blue, went on with life, undisturbed by spectres, and both Bituin and Beatriz simply went with that imperturbable flow, half-forgetting. The Monsantillos seemed to be very good at selective forgetting, and so was their house. In 1957, neither memory nor evidence remained of the lives that were sacrificed just for Hacienda Vida to even begin existing.

Whenever the Arguelleses would visit, they would experience an air of breezy simplicity, a feeling of calm that they did not really get in their own house of mazes and secrets, as if Hacienda Vida was never connected to any evil.

The Monsantillos were the ones closest to the Arguelleses, because they were the most alike. The Visbales, on the other hand, were the Monsatillos's opposite in way of life, attitude and general outlook. Everyone found the Visbales too perplexing, even unearthly, with their light hair and light eyes and light skins and their cloistered, hermitic stillness. They were tall and thin and slow and dolorous, walking under large parasols and under the shadows on the rare occasions that they walked outdoors. They stayed inside their house more often than not.

The Visbal house was built under a loose cluster of fully grown acacia trees, somewhere near the borders of their land, called Hacienda Dolores, in the town of Kamansi. The house was somehow designed and built to go around the cluster of giant trees, without disturbing them or taking any of them down. Thus, the layout of the house's innards was also irregular. Furthermore, inside the house, the dark and heavy drapes were always closed and the furniture was eternally permeated by the smell of camphor and rotting leaves. Even the occasional vase of flowers was not taken away until the flowers themselves had already wilted and dried. The very air inside was old and humid, causing the house itself to have the look and the ambience of a mausoleum. They managed their hacienda by employing the expertise of a group of envoys, attorneys, and business managers, never venturing to ride out to the fields themselves, but allowing their power to be countermanded by people not of their own blood and not of their own origins. This the other families found not only bizarre but wrong, even for the more contemporary-thinking Monsantillos.

But there it was, and Hacienda Dolores seemed to be doing relatively well, if it was to be judged by the fact that they had been able to retain their chosen lifestyle for years, without having to take loans from banks and without having to live stringently. So the Monsantillos and the Arguelleses begrudgingly accepted that perhaps for Hacienda Dolores, this was the perfect setup. However, their landholdings had not grown in over seventy years, and they had fewer family members now than a century and a half ago. Nevertheless, the three family stayed close together in spirit, characteristically dismissive of the more obscure details of their past, stuck together, more out of obligation and habit than out of choice. At the zenith of economic power in Camarines, there was no one else but the three of them. They were lonely at the top.

These three families clung together as the triumvirate of blood, wealth and power that kept Camarines in constant and abundant yield and its townspeople employed. These were the fruits of the partnerships, the alliances, the friendships, the inter-marriages, the lives and the years spent together in Camarines, but lurking underneath the glory were unpunished sins.

Chapter 4

The Maps of Camarines

Camarines was a province whose sprawling lands kept changing and shifting, like the house of the Arguelleses, over the years, upon the whims and desires and plans of a series of people. These people seemed always restless for something, always in search of something, of some form and order that could only be found by adding to what was already there, only to be eventually judged as either deficient or insufficient. This tortuous process served to create a huge web of halls and rooms and lines, and this was how the maps of Camarines, which did exist, kept changing over time.

The story behind the maps of Camarines was much larger than the story behind the ever-changing house of the Arguelleses, but both stories involved destruction. In 1571, the Spaniards, led by the Conquistador Juan de Salcedo, landed on a vast, rich and fertile land in Luzon, within the region called Bicol. For some reason, this land was territorially divided into two; so the Spaniards called it Ambos Camarines, to encompass both sides of the province, and treated the two as one. They all saw the many potentials of the place, not only the fecundity of the earth but also the opportunities that could be had from its long and meandering coastlines. Because of these, several Spaniards fought for ownership of the land, in the many ways they knew how: legally, politically, by fiduciary means, by right of first arrival, by one's proximity to the throne of Spain. But things were never settled. All the while, the lives of the natives went on as usual, as if the Spaniards were just a small and amusing nuisance, their presence and voices a means of entertainment to Bicolanos.

The Spaniards themselves seemed confused as to what to do with Camarines. They ran around surveying land and drawing up maps and writing up legislations that would fuse and then divide certain areas and districts over and over again, fusing and dividing, naming and renaming, fighting among themselves along the way. There seemed to be no true goal in sight, and no apparent leadership that would have given order to all the confusion.

The feuds went on, maps drawn, areas blocked off, placed under the name of one Spaniard and then another, and territorial lines overlapped. Hostilities escalated further, and maps were discarded and drawn and discarded again, as the escalation of the vendetta went on and on for years. Even when the parishes were put up, and the delineated territories were granted by royal decree to the friars as stewards, the haggling and the clashes continued among the Spanish *insulares*, a battle now involving the friars, who were often politically connected and had the advantage of actually being assigned to hold some powers over certain areas by the authority of the Spanish crown.

It was only after many of these Spaniards had given up and left Bicol for other territories and other islands that the newly married Sebastian Arguelles and his wife, Marianita Enojado, appeared, as if on cue, when Ambos Camarines was seemingly already free of the fighting, wrangling earlier Spaniards. It was 1784, and Ambos Camarines seemed an idyllic and almost infinite landscape in which to lay claim to land and raise a new family, far, far away from the convoluted politicking and family feuds in Spain. Sebastian, holding the most recent maps left by his exasperated and unsuccessful predecessors, decided that he wanted for his planned new hacienda the lands that were located mostly in the town of Toog. He aligned himself with the friars in Toog, who owned part of the land he wanted, wined and dined with them, donated money to their parishes, pledged to have convents built, and befriended them. Eventually, the friars were able to manipulate the Filipinos, who had been living on the adjoining lands long before the Spaniards came, to allow Sebastian to use their land. Rent was promised, and rent was given, but rent was never raised over the decades even though Hacienda Marianita grew, despite many requests made over time by the descendants of the original Filipino owners. Eventually it became almost negligible. However, the hacienda system was already deeply ingrained into the economic system of Toog, so they had no other alternative but to continue working for Sebastian. This was how Sebastian worked. He did not draw blood, but systematically and stealthily stole the rights of others.

The Arguelles name was known in Madrid, not as a part of the aristocracy or the nobility, but as a very old family of unknown origins that rose to fiscal power and had a ruthless reputation for acquiring land and property. They were also known for expanding their bloodline into families with superior political clout, and yet somehow, they were able to steer clear of anything that had to do with the Spanish royal line. The friars surmised that that was what these new Arguelleses were sent to Camarines for, hence their deferential manner in dealing with Sebastian. The friars did not want to get in the way of power of the kind that they did not quite understand because it did not emanate from the royal crown of Spain, so they gave in. And as Sebastian acquired the land he wanted, piece by piece, by promising things that he would eventually abandon, a new map of Camarines was drawn up, and that vast expanse of unbroken land was eventually labelled on the maps as 'Hacienda Marianita'.

Sebastian first rented a large but simple house that belonged to the Pansays in the area, for him and Margarita to live in temporarily while he built the very first incarnation of the Arguelles house. He designed it himself and had it built from the ground up. All the work was done within eight months, with the help of the Filipino masons and carpenters and craftsmen, helpfully procured by the friars and generously paid by Sebastian, because the finished house made him feel truly happy. Its windows were always wide open to the sun and breeze, the balconies always looked over the land that belonged to him, and Marianita and the servants made sure that everything in the house was neat, clean and beautiful, and with a system of management that was almost regimented in its style.

This was the house in which Marianita got pregnant and gave birth to Enrique, the very first true-blooded Arguelles that was born on Camarines soil, an *insulares*. His christening was considered a momentous affair and was attended by most of the important figures in the political, business, ministerial society of Camarines. Sebastian presided over the reception and declared Enrique to be the very first Arguelles that would grow up knowing Camarines as his one and only true home and treat it as such. Marianita, carrying her son in her arms in his long, embroidered christening gown, was understandably proud, but she was also deeply unhappy. She knew nothing of what was to become of her, but for the moment, Hacienda Marianita flourished, and Enrique grew up and learnt how to walk and to mumble phrases both in Spanish and Bicol, and Marianita chose to be cheerful and happy, and to ignore things that she didn't understand, including the harshness that Sebastian had begun treating her with. Sebastian, more powerful than ever, was the *hidalgo* that no one could destroy, and Marianita felt it was not her place to question any of his methods.

Two years later, when the hacienda itself had already consistently yielded substantial produce, signs that the land was indeed fertile, Sebastian received a letter from Jaimito Monsantillo, an old friend of the Arguelleses. Jaimito said in the letter that his wife, Vida Toledano, had died three months prior, and his emotional and mental state at the moment was not conducive for the many stealthy and deceptive business dealings that he used to thrive on in Madrid. The Monsantillos managed large farms in Spain that yielded an assortment of produce like fruits, corn, fish and a variety of vegetables, and were generally successful, but still not exempt from politicking and land-grabbing, as many other businessmen there were subjected to. Jaimito, in his letter, wanted to know if there was an opportunity for him to start again with a new life in Camarines, with his eight small children and Vida's two unmarried sisters.

Sebastian did not mind helping Jaimito out, but he also did not want to share the land that he had worked so hard to acquire. However, he immediately took out his maps of Camarines and decided that a large swathe of land in the town of Mangkono would be good for Jaimito to start a new life with his family. That these lands were already owned by generations of Filipinos was irrelevant to Sebastian.

Next he went out to see the friars in the area. By this time, he had already created a good reputation for himself because of Hacienda Marianita, which by now had begun to be a burgeoning territory that gave employment to many natives and gave much yield that made Camarines one of the most bountiful areas in the country. The friars in Mangkono, just like the friars in Toog, could not say no. Sebastian's next move, then, was to send a letter to Jaimito, telling him to take his family and set sail for the Las Islas Filipinas immediately, because the land was already waiting for him in the Camarines.

And so Jaimito arrived, his entire weary and disoriented brood in tow. His family stayed in the Arguelleses house, while Jaimito and Sebastian worked to arrange for the acquisition of the lands, and for a while, the house was a bit more difficult to manage for Marianita. But she was an understanding soul who could see that the Monsantillos were still in mourning, although they thought they were already free of it by sailing to Camarines. But the truth about death is that the dead are never really dead. Death follows one wherever one goes, and sets up house in one's heart and lives there forever. One is left with only a part of one's heart available for the rest of their time in this world. And so Marianita was patient and kind to these eight small children and two sisters of the dead Vida Toledano, knowing they would have only a part of their hearts functioning for the rest of their lives. This propensity to understand too much of others eventually became the catalyst for her own destruction.

In the meantime, Jaimito, together with Sebastian, transacted with the friars and were successful in inviting them to the usual scheme. It was Sebastian who did the bulk of the negotiations and Jaimito merely acceded, for he was truly not in the right frame of mind to make serious decisions with lasting results for his family, his faculties having been somehow weakened temporarily by the death of Vida. He was grateful for Sebastian, and took his cues from him. Agreements were made, papers were signed, rent was promised, and a new map of Camarines was drawn once more.

Such were the circumstances that changed the face of Camarines, not just on paper, but with the terrain itself. Although part of Jaimito's land was already on the supposed other side of Ambos Camarines, for all intents and purposes, the two families considered their separate haciendas as part of one and the same ancestry and traditions, pitched on the selfsame soil, and so none of them ever called the place Ambos Camarines. In their obstinate, Spanish hearts, there was only one Camarines, and it belonged to them.

The Visbales came to the country much later, after the unsolved death of Joselito, the twenty-two-year-old first-born son of Federico Visbal and Narcisa Santa Ana, who was found by a servant one morning in his bed, in his own bedroom, with forty-three stab wounds all over his body. The window was found open, letting in the cold, crisp air of Madrid, and there were signs of a struggle, although the thick carpets and heavy masonry of the walls prevented much of the scrimmage from being heard by anyone outside the room. The bed linens have been flung around in the struggle, and it was apparent that the killer had found Joselito to be already in bed by the time he had gotten in through the window.

Investigations pointed to vengeance against the family as a motive, since the Visbales, being businessmen, did not always resort to honest and scrupulous business practices. All businessmen at some point in their lives have had to be callous in some way or another, and as a result of this necessary evil, the safety of their family shall have to depend on whom the family was being dishonest with. A family just as ruthless would almost always resort to some form of vengeance, but the Visbales were not expecting this kind of brutality.

Yet they had so many enemies in the world of trade and business that it was difficult to pinpoint who had ordered Joselito killed. Eventually, they decided to contact Sebastian Arguelles and Jaimito Monsantillo, who they heard were doing well in a more benevolent country, with people much more servile than the impetuous Spanish. They asked if the entire remaining family of the Visbales—Federico, Narcisa, and their four remaining younger children, Eva, Estrella, Cecilia, and Federico II, and a few servants, could be assisted for a safe passage to Las Islas Filipinas.

Sebastian and Jaimito, upon receipt of the letter from the Visbales, put their heads together and tried to find land for the Visbales in Camarines. They were able to pinpoint the last remaining untitled strip of land from the end of the Arguelles land, which was in the town named Kamansi. When Federico Visbal and his family arrived in Camarines, they were weary, grieving and terrified that a murderer could be at their heels and could kill them all at any moment. Both Sebastian and Jaimito saw that Federico was not in the proper state to transact about land ownership. He was nervous, distraught, had a terrible cough and could not stand cool temperatures, so he kept to his bedroom. He looked much older than his forty-six years. To the other two Spaniards, he already looked to be almost sixty. So the two took it upon themselves to transact with the friars themselves on behalf of Federico, and just like before, agreements were made, this time in Kamansi, and did not meet much resistance.

It was Narcisa who declared, in a sombre voice one evening at dinner, when both Sebastian and Jaimito brought the good news that their land was to be named Hacienda Dolores, which is the Spanish word for 'sorrows', as if deciding that their entire land, only newly acquired, was to be in constant mourning. And so a new map of Camarines was drawn up, and the borders of Hacienda Dolores were delineated from among the territorial lines of the other three haciendas. This was the map of Camarines that was in effect for the longest time, even after the Spanish–American War, even after the friars had left, even after the Commonwealth Government was set up and Manuel L. Quezon, the very first Filipino

President, was appointed to head the country, and until the end of the Commonwealth in 1946. It was the longest-living map of Camarines, and in it, the three haciendas could be seen to hold sway over everything—Hacienda Marianita with the huge, irregular house and the rolling hills and the lakes, Hacienda Vida, with the plains and the varieties of its plantations, and Hacienda Dolores, covering the northernmost part of the province, with its shadowy plains and forests. These shadowy terrains, perhaps, was what set the tone for the kind of life the Visbales would eventually live in Camarines, and what had sealed their fate, their glory, and then their collapse, which were forever intertwined, since time immemorial, with that of the other two families.

Toog, where the Arguelles lands are, has a total land area of about eighty-five square kilometres, fifty-one square kilometres of which was Hacienda Marianita. The remaining land area belonged to the friars and the government, and some long, thin stretches along the meandering coast were left to the fisherfolk and their communities. Most of Toog lands in the time of Jacobo and his family were devoted to the farming of palay and abaca, with smaller sections of land used to grow sugarcane. Paddy fields and abaca plantations of Hacienda Marianita spanned nineteen of the twenty-six different barangays of Toog, a rather sprawling enterprise, but it was nevertheless highly organized. The two different kinds of farms were separately managed, with the rice fields and the abaca plantation each having their own *encargado*. Each encargado is in charge of managing and overseeing the daily operations of the farms in each and every barangay, which includes planting, cultivation, harvesting and processing of the crops, and then the eventual turnover to distribution. The payment of the wages of the farm workers also fell on the shoulders of the encargados.

Palay was grown in cycles of about four months each, after which time the harvested palay was milled to make rice. The paddies, made of compacted mud and small rocks and held together with grass, were usually laid out in a grid of fifteen metre square, their border dikes high enough and thick enough to sustain water that's five centimetres deep. The paddies of Hacienda Marianita were planned and executed with almost surgical precision, and turned out to be very aesthetically pleasing, rivalling most street plans and street maps in European cities at the time. That precision was one of the many things that Sebastian Arguelles brought with him to Camarines, and one that he insisted on at all times, until the day he died. Almost all of his male descendants were taught this precision, which helped them in their business, but not in their respective marriages.

The operation of the palay farms, too, was managed like clockwork in Hacienda Marianita, regardless of the weather. Palay was known to be traditionally fragile in inclement weather, and Camarines was known to have torrential typhoons all year round, although the bulk of the typhoons usually happened in the months of June through August.

The smaller farms experience heavy losses during typhoons, and more often than not, during the typhoon season, they simply decide not to bother planting rice at all, but Sebastian had devised efficient systems to mitigate the loss of harvest during these typhoons. Thus, all year-round, the palay farms of Hacienda Marianita were always in different stages of cultivation, in graduated shades of green and graduated stalk heights, in a perfectly laid, uninterrupted grid work as far as the eyes could see, with Mount Isarog as the backdrop. Even the fallow land that needed to be alternately left alone for one planting season managed to look rich and promising, as if the land itself was fully aware of their upcoming planting schedule and it need not look despondent. And even when the almost-ripe stalks were forcibly bent near their base to lie on the ground while weathering a typhoon, to prevent loss of the grains in wind speeds of between ninety and one hundred and ninety kilometres per hour, they were done in a slant against the watery mud, as if dissecting the grid diagonally, but more or less along the forecasted direction of the wind when the typhoon would pass through Camarines. From Sebastian's precise hands to Jacobo's, the system of management changed very little, as there was little that needed changing from Sebastian's original methods.

Apolonio was Jacobo's encargado in the palay farm at Barangay Ilawod. He was forty-five, unmarried, but deeply in love with Filomena, a woman who was fifty and had three husbands and thirteen sons with ages ranging from four to thirty-four. Her third husband was also thirty-four. Her second husband was fifty-one, and worked as a rice mill operator in the town poblacion. Her first husband, sixty-two, was a clerk at the municipio. Her third husband, the one that was the same age as her oldest son, was a handsome drunkard. All three husbands lived with her and her thirteen sons in a house with six bedrooms, three kitchens and two outhouses.

Apolonio, on the other hand, had been living alone since his mother died almost a decade ago, in a small, three-bedroom cottage made of stone. His father was the Arguelles encargado in Ilawod before him, as was his father's father. His family had known no employer beyond the Arguelleses, and the same can be said for most of the families who lived in Barangay Ilawod. Apolonio devoted his days to the palay farm in Ilawod, and his nights to Filomena who, because of the constant cacophony that was her enormous and chaotic household, could escape forthwith for several hours unnoticed. Any one of her husbands would just assume she was with one of the other two, and her

children had always been left to their own devices, including
the four-year-old and the seven-year-old, who were assigned
to be cared for by the eleven-year-old and the twelve-year-old,
respectively. The cooking and the cleaning were assigned to the
older sons, while the rest of the sons just staggered in and out of
the house randomly, in various levels of wretchedness, jubilation,
mania, or rage. None of the sons ever attended school. None of
the sons old enough to work had been employed by anyone
for longer than a month. When they needed money for any of
their miscreant needs, they would haul sacks of palay or rice for
the rice mills for a day or two. The first and second husbands
financed only the household's legitimate needs, but it remained
a mystery as to how the third husband was able to finance his
own lifestyle.

Apolonio was normally a level-headed person, used to the
eternal routine that generations of encargados had enforced
in the farms, but for the past month that routine had been
increasingly disturbed by several workers complaining about
what they claimed were unfairly low wages. Apolonio himself
did not agree, because they were being paid the same as they had
been for years and their work never changed. He nevertheless
brought up the matter with Jacobo, who seemed like he was
listening, but did not reply that day, and did not reply on any
other day after that. The workers, in turn, continued to ply
Apolonio with the matter, becoming more and more agitated
as the days went by without receiving any response from Jacobo.

Apolonio did not like this disturbance in his placid,
predictable life, but he was well aware that the solution did
not lie in his hands, so to escape from the seeming impasse he
needed Filomena more and more often. He used to be fine with
her leaving to go back to her overpopulated home at midnight,
but now he only let her go home before dawn. At first, Filomena
resisted, using her youngest sons as an excuse, but Apolonio

knew she never took care of them, so her resistance was easy for him to protest against. Eventually Filomena herself had grown accustomed to staying at his house until right before the sun rose, and it seemed that her own household never even noticed that she wasn't home most nights. And while their nights were relatively contained thusly, and while the Arguelleses's nights were even more undisturbed by matters that they did not consider a problem or even just something that deserved their attention, an upheaval, which had throbbed itself into life long ago, first taking root in shallow ground, then lengthening its tendrils to begin entwining with what had been there long before them, shot up out of the ground.

Chapter 5

Harvest

But if the destined ruination of the three families were ever to happen, as such things almost always eventually do, it would not be during the summer of 1957, which was a golden year for Camarines. The Philippine government had already been experiencing true national freedom after the end of the Commonwealth Government in 1946. By this time, former President Ramon Magsaysay had already successfully vanquished the Huk rebellion in Central Luzon, which did not affect Camarines much.

The country was going through a stage of happy anticipation after the election and appointment of Carlos P. Garcia as the new President, serendipitously in the summer of 1957. His new administration created agencies for the main purpose of helping the masses, and for many people, this gave ample liberties and privileges to those who dreamt big and had the drive to succeed in life. This was also a time when government service was considered a noble profession to be in, and most of the working class felt that the fairness and justice that existed in their lives were caused by an efficient and trustworthy government. As if mirroring the overall environment of fairness and justice, yields from the various plantations and processing plants of the three different families had been very productive this summer.

The children, oblivious to the economics and politics that gave power to Camarines, simply enjoyed the fact that school was out, and they stayed in their bedrooms until mid-morning, had their breakfasts brought to them in bed, or even slept all day. In the afternoons they would go riding in their bicycles and would sometimes ride the horses to the banks of the irrigation to have lunch there.

Esperanza would enjoy to the hilt her annual ecstasy at being free of the Dominican nuns that she believed were the bane of her life in Colegio de Santa Rita. Inez and Paz, who went to the same school, could not care less. Their interests were the same whether or not school was out for the year. Guadalupe seemed to have no opinion or feelings on the matter, and kept to her needlework and her prayers. As per family tradition, ever since Jacobo II started studying at the seminario at thirteen, he would always go back to Hacienda Marianita for a two-month-long summer vacation.

The Semana Santa, also happening every summer, and usually during the most scorching part of the season, was part of a long tradition that began when the Spaniards arrived in Las Islas Filipinas. Before the Spaniards, the natives worshipped an assortment of deities for an assortment of needs, and had customs and practices that the Spaniards did not quite understand. The Spaniards considered the natives pagans, and heartily took the opportunity to convert them to Christianity. They had been mostly successful, except that the ancient mindset remained.

Over the years, as the two different societies sought to coexist with each other, there emerged an intense and rich culture that combined precolonial Filipino folklore and superstition with Spanish traditions and institutional mandates. Hence the people of Camarines, especially those who were born into non-Spanish families, believed in the existence of beings belonging to the underworld that were vengeful, gory, violent, horrific and very visible. At the same time, they also believed in the second-hand teachings of the more psychological kind, such as invisible entities and barely-there apparitions, brought by inescapable feelings of doom, all of which were summoned by a guilty conscience. This conscience was, of course, Spanish in nature, rooted in Spanish-sanctioned Roman Catholicism, and regulated by Spanish dogma.

The annual Semana Santa was a chance for all Roman Catholics in the country to examine their now-fused two kinds of consciences and repent for the sins they had committed. This was the symbolic week in which Jesucristo had suffered and died centuries ago in order to absolve all mankind of their sins. In the period between three o'clock in the afternoon of Viernes Santo and the dawn of Domingo de Pascua, the entire Roman Catholic world would be in mourning. In Camarines, with its continuing faith in ancient folklore, people believed that this was also the time when all the dregs of the earth, the creatures of the underworld, would come out and try to wreak havoc on the faith of the faithful, and further drag down the faithless into hell.

The people of Camarines would then show their faith in the most exaggerated of ways. Some men would allow themselves to be crucified on a cross much like Jesucristo had been. Real nails and crowns made with real thorns were used. For the less brave there was much praying of the santisimo rosario, much setting up of altars in the middle of their houses and altars outside their houses along the roads, and the visita altares, which is the visiting of the nearby churches just to say the same prayers over and over again. There was also much kneel-walking from the front door of the church to the altar, and hours spent lying down on the floor of the church, face down, arms splayed out like that of the crucified Jesucristo, while mumbling still more prayers.

There would also be a long, long line of penitents in front of the confessional boxes, in which overtaxed priests, drowsy in the blistering heat, would try to stay awake and listen to the various sins of the supposed faithful. These sins spanned from lying about money to stealing a chicken to copulating with the neighbour's wife. The priests yawned, pronounced their penalties, and declared forgiveness by the powers vested on them by the Santo Papa.

The Churches of Camarines were very old, grandly designed and built, but poorly ventilated. In the people's earnest, fervent, and sincere desire to be declared free of sin by the time Jesucristo rose from the dead, they contorted themselves into bizarre bodily positions while repeating the same orations over and over again. But while the faithful seemed to be in the throes of the agony of pleading for the salvation of their souls, all the images of the saints, the angels, the crucified Jesucristo, the Holy Sacrament, and all representations of heaven were veiled in black cloth. The saints were not even witness to this overt display of pious and repentant agony.

Being ardent Roman Catholics, the Arguelleses didn't mind being subjected to the same consideration as the sinful masses once a year. Mercedes, in her characteristic purple dress with a matching purple veil, kneeled all morning in front of the church's own image of the La Virgen de Guadalupe, which was completely veiled in black cloth, with her granddaughter Guadalupe by her side, praying the novena to the image as well as all three mysteries of the rosary in honour of their devotion. Margarita and Jacobo, with Esperanza, Jacobo II, Inez, and Paz in tow, prayed the Way of the Cross in the parish church. They prayed each prayer from the booklet in front of the appropriate painting in the series of paintings that hung on the high walls of the church, the only religious icons that were left unveiled, since the honouring of the passion and death of Jesucristo was the very purpose of Semana Santa. Assumpta had not yet turned eight, which was the age of First Holy Communion, and this exempted her from her divine duties this one final summer.

Semana Santa was also the time in which the life-sized statues of the many saints that the families of Camarines kept in their private prayer rooms would be paraded around the towns on wheeled platforms bedecked with flowers and lights. The saints would be taken out from where they stood for most of the year, wiped clean, dusted, their long, almost floor-length curly hairs shampooed dried, combed, and then re-curled. These would all be performed by female servants, to preserve the dignity and integrity of the female saints, and it would be the male servants who would clean up and ready the male saints for the procession. New vestments would be made for all the saints for the occasion. In the Arguelles house, Mercedes would head the design and the sewing of the vestments, who always clad La Virgen de Guadalupe, to whom she had a long-standing devotion, in majestic purple and gold. This year was no exception, except that Mercedes would be working closely together with her favourite granddaughter, Guadalupe, on this project. Aside from lending La Virgen de Guadalupe, the Arguelleses also lent Maria Jacobe and Maria Salome, which were added to the parade of saints in Toog.

Each Viernes Santo parade would begin in the parish church, go around the main streets of the town, and end in the same church. The parish priest and his sacristans would lead the procession of life-sized saints, and the congregation would follow along the sides and the back of the row of saints. All throughout the pageant, people would sing songs of devotion, incantations of the greatness of the Lord, and pleas for the forgiveness of souls, the repose of the faithful already departed, and the eventual release of the souls still trapped in Purgatory by decree of the level of their sins, still in the process of earning their way into heaven.

Behind this glorified row of immutable, inviolate saints walked men wearing black hoods and black short pants, their torsos naked. They walked barefoot and wordlessly in a slow cadence to the beat of a single drum, while striking their own bare backs in time with short whips made out of a bunch of ropes with spikes at the end. These were the *flagellantes*, men who chose to undergo what Jesucristo went through as he was scourged at the pillars. Many of these men had been flagellantes for a long time, and many had backs that had been hardened by the callouses that the scars of the whips had caused over time. The congregation tried to steer clear of the flagellantes, because streams and droplets of blood would lash out from among the men and stain their clothing. Some of the new flagellantes would faint and be brought to the nearest hospital, but many of them managed to last until the end of the Parade of Saints before being rushed to the hospital themselves.

The Arguelleses would often watch this grotesque display of repentance and faith from the front balcony of the municipal hall of Toog, which gives the best view of the parade. Since the Arguelleses were the most prominent family of the town, the mayor would invite them to this every year. The balcony would turn into an ostentatious display of piety and righteousness, where the invited guests would try to out-holy everyone else by quoting scripture every chance they got. The Arguelles children were more enraptured by the parade, which looked far less holy and saintlike than what their studies had exposed them to. They would watch with big eyes as the morbid, bloody procession of symbols of death marched by in agonizing slowness. When the macabre display ended, everyone would walk down the stairs silently and walk just as silently with the people at the end of the parade, towards the parish church a few hundred metres away. The Holy Mass that capped the event was celebrated by the parish priest, with a sermon made pointedly long for the occasion, and which focused on the dogma that everyone was born a sinner.

The next day, which would be Sabado de Gloria, everyone would have to be up early. On this day, while Jesucristo was still considered dead, there was the tradition of singing the Pasion, a book-length mournful dirge that chronicled the life, passion, death, and resurrection of Jesucristo. This was an intoned incantation that would last the entire Sabado de Gloria, starting from five o'clock in the morning until four o'clock in the afternoon. There were three versions of the Pasion in Camarines: one was in the Bicol language, another one was in the language of the Tagalogs, and a third one was in Spanish. Naturally, the Arguelleses chose to meditate to the Spanish Pasion, which was traditionally sung by Tiang Tiray, an ancient woman with extremely bowed legs who was adopted by the Arguelleses a few generations ago and was still inexplicably alive and knew how to read but couldn't understand Spanish. That most of the servants didn't understand Spanish was not a problem for the Arguelleses; the story of Jesucristo was the same regardless of what language was used to tell it.

During the entire time, every member of the family, and all servants, were to be in the same room where the Pasion was being held, and all were required to stay still and meditate on Jesucristo's ultimate sacrifice. The members of the family would sit bolt upright in upholstered chairs in front of the altar, behind Tiyang Tiray. The servants would be a metre or two behind, sitting in rows of ordinary chairs brought up from the kitchen and the servants' quarters. Everyone would sit still, supposedly listening to Tiyang Tiray and the profundity of the words she was reading. All of the servants knew that Tiyang Tiray could not understand a word of Spanish, and neither could they, and the family they served could not really care less about such a detail, as long as the tradition was followed, and the ritual was performed as it was supposed to. But the truth is that during the Pasion, everyone's minds, from time to time, wandered far from the Pasion, and Assumpta's, expectedly, travelled the farthest. Her mind was eternally on the maps that existed in her secret world, a world of drawings and paper and delineations between territories, maps that were also bearers of names of people and places. In Assumpta's secret world, all that existed were existing because they were written down on paper.

During Semana Santa, all work in the haciendas was placed on halt, as it has always been since the time of Sebastian. The workers, in turn, were required to follow the tenets of the Roman Catholic Church in observing the traditions and processes that are required for the week, which were actually quite simple, even formulaic. But because of the more macabre ancient Filipino culture underlying every native in Camarines, Semana Santa had become a time for the emergence of ghouls, and all sorts of aswang, beings both monstrous and ugly. Said to be equally active in this period were dwarves who hurled curses if one didn't give them what they wanted, and it is said that all poisonous snakes and reptiles, in the stifling heat of the summer, would slither out of their burrows and strike any living creature they saw nearby, humans not exempted.

But the most important presence in the Semana Santa is not the presence of the Roman Catholic tradition. Instead, this week, the human conscience took centre stage, and it always appeared in people's hearts with a fury, all light and luminosity. This placed people on some kind of otherworldly edge. And when one is acting on an imposed, precise and pedantic conscience, and when one has secrets, as everyone in the Arguelles family did, guilt rises to the surface of their deep, ancient, family hearts.

Margarita, knowing that she was guilty of keeping her body and her heart distant from Jacobo, the man she professed to love and obey till death did them part, was wracked with guilt, and could not eat normally, so she had grown into proportions that would not possibly allow Jacobo into her bed even if they both wanted to. In her hunger for a strange, numbing forgiveness, which she felt helpless to satiate, she saw the image of the *multong fantasma* twice during Semana Santa this year. The multong fantasma stood in a corner of her bedroom, by the drapes, his very long and very thin form dressed in a pure white shirt, with his pants a deep black, fading just above the floor. His face was also abnormally long and thin, and in his rheumy eyes, Margarita could see an accusation that she had been amiss in her duties and in her faith, and that she shall be judged as such. Margarita stayed where she was, looking back at the multong fantasma with a blank face but a fiercely beating heart, until the apparition went away.

Mercedes, knowing what went on in the house years and years before, was also exceptionally guilty during Semana Santa. She knew about some of the crimes that were planned, and in certain instances committed, inside the house, but she kept her peace, not saying a word to anyone, not to the police, not to the priest in the confessional box, for as many Semana Santas as she could remember. Mercedes during Semana Santa was silence incarnate.

Her guilt was for the crime of omission, and each year she awaited the sense of doom in her heart that was the harbinger of, first, a sound of chains being rattled, and then of a very hard object being dragged across the floorboards, and then, through the periphery of her vision, she would see the multong condenado, an ancient, filthy man, bent under the weight of his sins, condemned to roam the halls of a guilty forever, without peace or mercy, not unlike Mercedes, who had decided to carry the burdens of her secret for as long as she was alive, to protect the family name and power. Both these women kept the apparition to themselves, as was the habit of all Arguelleses.

What everyone truly looked forward to during Semana Santa was the end of it, specifically Domingo de Pascua, when Jesucristo has already risen from the dead, and everyone has been, for all intents and purposes, saved from sin. Finally, after a week of austerity and unnatural quietude in the house, in which they could not even eat their favourite meat *viands*, and the horrors of the night of Sabado de Gloria, they could go back to living their lives as normal. Also, the muggy, oppressive heat that usually pervaded the summer of Camarines and rose to an all-time high during Semana Santa, would usually begin to die down, bringing forth fresher breezes from the hills and the forests and dainty, delicate May showers, which marked the beginning of the rainy season. A May shower was one of those light, sheer drizzles that had the texture of lacework through which the distance could be seen like a vague, shimmering painting. It barely made a sound on the thick grass of the fields, and made a delicate sound as the tiny raindrops fell on the rooftop of the house.

At some point, the rain, at first diaphanous, would start to increase its intensity, eventually becoming grey and opaque, the much-fatter raindrops falling in torrents, obscuring anyone's view beyond a few feet. The mild staccato of the rain would increase, its once-hidden rage building up until it reached a crescendo that echoed even louder. When that happened, it ceased to be a May shower and officially became *Agua de Mayo*.

Agua de Mayo is supposedly the very first major rain of the season, and signalled the end of summer, and that was when the farmers of the haciendas would start to plant rice again. When the dry, cracked earth had given up its yield and bounty, the heavens opened up to drench the plains with water and then turned the dry, gritty soil into warm, fragrant mud, dark as dead dreams but fertile again, absorbent again, as a woman regenerates after childbirth.

Everyone welcomed the refreshing coolness. Every child in Camarines had the urge to suddenly run out into the rain, their arms outstretched, their eyes closed, and their mouths open to receive the waters from heaven. Assumpta would have loved to do the same, but she was not allowed to. Instead, she stayed indoors, exploring the grotesque house that was bursting with secrets and some inaudible heaving, until one afternoon, one hour into Agua de Mayo, she found herself on the fourth floor of Sebastian's tower, looking straight at the door to his locked, forbidden bedroom. She stood for a few minutes with her face aligned with the tarnished brass doorknob, and then blew at the thick layer of dust covering it. There was a keyhole underneath the doorknob but she could see nothing through it. She jiggled the doorknob, but nothing happened. She looked closely at the wood of the door and saw that the wood had warped over time. Sebastian's bedroom was the only room on this floor, and after he died, no one had any reason to come up here to check on the conditions of the door.

Assumpta trailed her fingers along one of the cracks on the door, her fingers slowly playing around with a whorl in the wood that looked a little like the face of Luningning's old husband, and then came to a rest at the midrail, which was at the same level as her head. The midrail had inlays made of darker-coloured wood, in a series of rectangles and squares, which were part of the design of the door, but because the wood had warped, some of these inlaid wood had become misaligned and some of them had begun to pop out. Assumpta started knocking on the inlays softly, one by one, imagining them to be miniature doors to miniature rooms where miniature fairies held office, granting people's wishes.

'Knock, knock,' Assumpta whispered to each door, each word uttered in time with the actual knocking of her knuckles. Each inlay sounded muffled when knocked on, and Assumpta made her way methodically through them, from left to right, but when she got nearer to the right, closer to where the doorknob was, the rectangular inlay there sounded hollow. She knocked on it again, and then knocked on the other inlays, just to be sure that there really was a different sound to that one inlay, and verified that this one really did sound hollow. She took one step back, and surveyed the entire door. There were also the same square and rectangular inlays on the top rail and the bottom rail. She could not reach the top rail, but she lay down on the floor, with her ear only an inch away from the door, to check the row of inlays at the bottom of the door. The floor was thick with dust, but Assumpta was never one to care about dust or how dirty she became. She knocked on each inlay at the bottom rail slowly and methodically, from left to right, and found that none of them sounded hollow.

She bolted straight up from the floor, and knocked once more at the inlay on the mid-rail that sounded hollow. Assumpta examined that specific inlay much closer, which was not very easy, as the only light available was coming from the windows that were to the left and to the right of her, and it was still raining very hard outside. She decided to feel around the borders of the inlay with her fingers, and began to pry it out with her short fingernails, but nothing happened, so, annoyed, she pushed on the entire inlay with the heel of her hand. She heard a metallic noise, faint against the continuing roar of the rain outside, and saw the inlay dislodge itself from out of its socket with a slight grating sound, further releasing even more dust.

The inlay was at the same level as her head, so to look behind it she had to raise her heels a little. She did, and then looked down. The inlay was a receptacle. It was made like a tiny drawer, not so deep, and inside the unlined and relatively clean interior of the receptacle lay one large key. Assumpta immediately knew what the key was for, and she thought it was a brilliant hiding place, which was why no one had ever found the key, according to some family stories she had heard, even in Sebastian's pockets, which people searched after he died. The key to the door was *inside* the door, just waiting for whoever would be either patient enough or curious enough to walk up the tower and look.

Assumpta took the key out of the drawer and pushed the inlay back in. It more or less blended back into its place with the same slight grating sound. She examined the key, which looked like the key illustrated in some of her fairytale books. The key was large and tubular and made of a dark metal, unlike the keys she often saw with Mercedes and Luningning, which were flat and shiny and silver and small. She put the end of the key into the keyhole, and she had to turn it left and right several times before she found the right angle of the key that would open the door, but when that happened, she heard a metallic thud, and saw the doorknob shake very slightly. She twisted the doorknob, slowly opened the door, and felt dank, cold air pass through her from the inside. She felt the floor heave, and then walked inside as she heard the rain beginning to die down.

That was how Assumpta had come across Sebastian's secrets, enclosed in a thin sheaf of papers, which she could not really understand because they were in some complicated Spanish, while her own Spanish was very rudimentary. But she had the papers now, and kept them in her secret hiding place together with her hand-drawn maps, which she had added to by drawing a map of the fourth floor. She spent most of the rainy season in her favourite room with the claw-foot bathtub, which, over the months after she had found it, she filled with some of the books from Jacobo's library, and she was quite comfortable reclining her small frame inside the large, hard, cold curves of the bathtub as she read. When it rained, hard and uproarious, she would look out the window and feel the cold wind rifle her hair and her dress, and circulate through the entire room, and feel the spray of the tumultuous rain dampen her face. All this while in the great outdoors, the rain revitalized the fields that had been dry for weeks due to the heat of the summer and caused more greenery to burst forth from trees and plants and other shrubberies, like so many new lives and so many new hopes. Indeed, if there was to happen a ruination of major proportions in Camarines, it would be later, not in the magnificent, golden summer of 1957.

Chapter 6

Dark Storms

In the Arguelles house, however, things were slightly discordant, but not due to anything of great magnitude. After a million aimless arguments between Margarita and Esperanza over a span of weeks, the day of the eighteen-year-old daughter's formal entrance into society loomed closer and closer, and culminated with news of an incoming typhoon that was scheduled to make landfall on the day of the soirée itself. The typhoon was named Luisa, and was forecast to have sustained winds of 135 kilometres per hour. This worried Esperanza to no end.

The tormented debutante barged into Mercedes's room and found the old woman by the window reading a book.

'Abuelita!' Esperanza ran to her and fell at her feet. 'It's a bad omen! A very bad omen! The typhoon is to arrive exactly tomorrow, of all days! Oh, how horrible!'

'It's just a typhoon, querida,' Mercedes sighed. Her acid tongue was reserved only for the servants, not for her family. 'We've had many typhoons before.'

'But not tomorrow!' Esperanza wailed. 'Not tomorrow of all days! It's my day! It's my day!'

'Hija, it's a typhoon, not a *cursillo*. It cannot be rescheduled.'

'But the entire setup will be ruined! Ruined! Oh!' Esperanza hopped up, tore at her long, curly dark brown hair, and walked around the room maniacally.

'No one will be able to go out into the gardens! The lights cannot be set up there! People will be slopping mud all over the carpets and rugs and the tiles!' Esperanza threw her hands over her head as she walked around Mercedes's bed, with Mercedes calmly looking at her, saying nothing, her face blank. 'Many might not even come because of this horrid typhoon! The streets will be flooded and no cars could get through!' She ran to the window, only half of it open, and gesticulated wildly at the darkening skies. 'And if a handful do end up making it, all windows will be closed against the typhoon, and the drapes will be closed to make people forget that we are amid a typhoon, and it will be as if we were having the debut at Hacienda Dolores!' She held her face in her hands, and her face looked so pained that Mercedes almost, *almost* felt sympathetic with her. 'Darkness and dead flowers, and cold air and all that! Oh, it's just so horrible! And what if there's a power outage? I'm dead!' She moved her hands up to her hair and rumpled her curls as if she was about to tear them out. 'My life is doomed! Doomed!'

After this litany, she threw herself on Mercedes's bed, rumpling the damask sheets and sobbing theatrically as if it were, indeed, the end of the world as she knew it.

Mercedes sighed even more deeply, her face still blank. She was certain that Margarita allowed Esperanza too much liberties, such as allowing her to watch too many Hollywood movies, which Mercedes considered inappropriate for the sensibilities of any grown girl from the family. Certainly the histrionics she was witnessing at the moment had happened before in a movie that the girl had seen.

Mercedes shook her head and continued reading her book while she waited for Esperanza to exit the room. Mercedes, with the wisdom gained after being an Arguelles for over seventy years, was certain that if anything were to ruin Esperanza's debut, it would not be this typhoon. It would be something far more quiet, but more demented and horrifying than any young Arguelles could ever imagine.

Margarita, on the other hand, steered clear of her wailing debutante for the day, and stayed downstairs in the kitchen, making sure the food would be ready in time. She took some of the servants with her, and they went around the ballroom to ensure that all windows would be sealed shut against the incoming typhoon, all drapes closed to keep out visions of dark wetness punctuated by flashes of lightning and anything else that would remind the guests that this was not a day to be in another family's house. She also ordered more lamps to be brought in, and some lights originally meant to decorate the inner courtyard were brought in to be placed at the backs of sofas and tables to provide more warm, ambient lighting for the entire ballroom. She hoped these would keep out the feeling of cold and wetness from which the guests would be coming in.

She also had as many candelabra as possible taken out of storage, polished, and placed on as many surfaces as possible, in case of a power outage. Candles of pink and white were procured in town, and the servants tasked to do it had to go through several stores just to complete the needed quantity and colour, since everyone else in town was also preparing for the typhoon and so candles were in short supply. But still, by some miracle, the candles were procured, and then pierced into the holders, ready to be lighted in case the typhoon got worse and toppled the electric lines. Many of the candelabra didn't match, and many looked to be much older than Mercedes, but Margarita felt, especially after they have been polished to a very high shine, that they added to the appeal of the setup.

She stood back to survey the results of her efforts, and then walked out of the ballroom, passed by the *sala*, and overheard Esperanza complaining about the typhoon, most likely to poor Sofia, whom Margarita was sure Esperanza must have already worn down like the rest of them. Then she went upstairs with Luningning, the majordoma, to check on the outfits to be worn by everyone. Assumpta was to wear a pink organza dress with a large bow at the back. Paz was to wear yellow in a similar cut. Inez was to wear a long, green dress with long bell sleeves that would hide the bruises and scratches on her arms and legs that she constantly sustained while romping about in the fields and the hills, climbing things and falling from them. Guadalupe was to wear powder blue. Both Jacobo and Jacobo II would be wearing white tie, and Mercedes was to wear purple, as always, but she had a new gown made especially for the occasion. Margarita was to wear scarlet velvet.

Margarita then went to Esperanza's room, and her daughter's debutante gown was truly a sight to behold. The skirt was a combination of taffeta, organza and chiffon, assembled as if by magic to flow through each other like a wide spiral, in varying intensities and shades of very pale pink. The bodice was made of silk, with a Sabrina neckline and elbow-length sleeves. The dress made her look like a dream, and Margarita was proud of the spectacle that she knew her daughter would make gliding down the main staircase while the guests looked up at her as if she was a goddess that had come down to earth. And as the mother of this debutante, Margarita worked hard in her heart to dismiss, or at least muffle, the portents that she felt in her soul once more.

As finally decided after days of harrowing debate, Esperanza would be wearing her hair in a chignon. She would be wearing Esmeralda's diamond tiara, earrings with large diamonds in a rositas setting, a matching ring on a finger of her left hand, and a thick cuff encrusted with white and pink diamonds on her left wrist.

All the Arguelles women would be bedecked with jewels, jewels that did not belong to them personally, though some had been made for them. By some ancient Arguelles decree, all jewellery, no matter who it was made and designed for, was to be considered part of the family estate and treated as part of its assets, not personal property of each member. Accountants and lawyers managed the inventories of these jewellery as they grew in volume, because the Arguelles women kept buying them and having them made over the years. They were kept in safe deposit boxes in two different banks in Camarines, to which only Mercedes and Jacobo had official access. On the day before Esperanza's debut, Mercedes went and took out all the jewellery chosen to be worn, and by evening they were all clean and gleaming after being polished by Luningning.

Luningning had been in the house at Hacienda Marianita for well over fifty years. She started service with the family at the age of ten after the death of her mother, the old cook. At first she was relegated to the kitchens, stirring concoctions before they were to be cooked, minding the fires and monitoring the time some dishes had to be taken out of the fire or turned over or adjusted to simmer. And then, when Mercedes saw that she exhibited loyalty, honesty, a strange ability to anticipate the needs of her masters and the astounding ability to be silent about the inexplicable things she has heard and witnessed inside the house, Mercedes made Luningning her own servant, so she could be trained on how to eventually run a household. Luningning was then sixteen years old.

Mercedes's characteristic acid tongue seemed to have had no adverse effect on the young woman. Mercedes also observed that Luningning had a penchant for being submissive and quiet with her masters while being consistently stern yet fair with the other servants, which made her a very good candidate for a majordoma. The servants liked and respected Luningning, and the last thing Mercedes wanted was an unruly set of servants.

The majordoma at the time, Pinyas, was already ancient and turning blind. Pinyas was the majordoma when Mercedes had arrived in Hacienda Marianita, and no one knew exactly how old she was. But when Pinyas finally died, all shrivelled and much smaller in death than in life that she required the casket that was made for a child, Luningning was twenty-seven years old and was promptly made majordoma.

Luningning cleaned and polished the jewellery the way Mercedes had taught her many years ago. The diamonds were not much of a problem after having been kept in their respective cases for a long time. They just needed gentle polishing after being soaked in a cleaning solution, and she needed to make sure that all the stones were complete in their settings. It was the pearls that had accumulated a powdery substance; so they needed to be rubbed with a bit of salt partially dissolved in water, and then dried and coated in oil. After that they had to be buffed with a soft cloth, so they could show their deep lustre.

The pearls that she was polishing at the moment belonged to Marianita Enojado. These were the pearls that she wore to her wedding to Sebastian in Spain, and they were commissioned specially for her by Sebastian himself. The set consisted of earrings with a single large perfectly round and white pearl each, a three-strand necklace with a yoke shaped like a large butterfly and heavily encrusted with pearls of different sizes but still perfectly white and round, a matching ring, and a heavy bracelet that matched the butterfly design of the necklace. This was the only set of jewellery that she brought with her to Camarines.

This pearl set became the seed from which the family's cache of jewellery grew, and throughout all the important events that the family attended, in which they were bedecked with jewels, no one had ever worn or even touched Marianita's pearls, except for Esmeralda, the mother of Antonio Arguelles, the grandmother of Alfonso Arguelles, the great-grandmother of Jacobo, and the great-great-grandmother of Jacobo's children. Esmeralda wore the pearls on the day of christening of Juancho, one of her grandsons. She died three days after that. Now those pearls, the very last set of the jewellery that had touched Esmeralda's skin before she died, had been brought out into the light, after being ensconced in their velvet-lined leather case, untouched, for many years.

They were to be worn by Mercedes. After several sleepless nights, in which Mercedes had felt a deep and eerie sense of dread, which grew stronger each day, she began to feel an undeniable conviction that Esperanza's debut would be the last debut that she would witness in her life. There was also one morning, at dawn, when the light was still fighting the darkness for its right to be in power for the day, that Mercedes could see a very faint outline of a woman by the window farthest from her bed. She recognized that woman to be Esmeralda Arguelles, whom she knew only from her portrait that had always been displayed in the ballroom of the house. The incident happened only once, but she knew it wasn't a dream, and there remained in her a foreboding feeling of the very first warning that the house had whispered into her ear the very first time she had walked through the threshold.

Mercedes had begun to assume that the house had seen how she had been true and loyal to the Arguelles blood to which she belonged by law and not by birth, by having kept its secrets for as long as she had. Thus, she somehow felt that her reward would be a final unburdening, which was why she brought

Marianita's pearls out of the safe deposit box. No one in the family questioned her choice. Perhaps, from within that deep, intense, powerful gene that runs through their veins, they already knew the reasons for Mercedes's decision, and from the abyss in which lay their ancient, beating hearts, they were strangely relieved for her. Even Luningning, herself a kind of incidental extended repository of the burdens of Mercedes's destiny, and completely sympathetic to the family's circumstances, applied herself to the meticulous task at hand. While carefully wiping Marianita's pearls, she mumbled prayers and pleas to Santa Maria, Madre de Dios, asking her to allow Mercedes the peace that she deserved after so many years of silence.

So everything was ready for the grand soirée, but as stated in the weather forecasts, Esperanza's eighteenth birthday was welcomed by a dark, cold, rainy morning that promised to be worse later on, and was expected to be at its worse on that very night. Surprisingly, almost all of the guests still agreed to come, even the reclusive Visbales. So the display was irrevocably on, and events and people had no choice but to move forward, as things often are in the heavy, ancient, intricate wheel of destiny that controls such families.

On the night of Esperanza's debut, in the hills and valleys, forests, swamplands and fields of palay and abaca and sugarcane that comprised the whole of Camarines, the typhoon raged on with liberation. Water fell in torrents, the wind howled and shrieked, and many trees and bushes had no choice but to fall in the direction of the wind and the water. Typhoon Luisa has arrived.

In the town, water began to overflow in the gutters and the canals, and some streets became flooded. Store owners closed their shops for the day, the windows held tight against the wind and rain by rope and sheets of either thick cardboard or corrugated metal, a precaution to protect glass window panes from breaking. Water seeped in through cracks in badly maintained houses and buildings. In the storage houses, stocks of rice and food and other supplies had to be moved to the higher parts of the storage area, in lofts, and upon platforms built by stacking crates upon each other. People worked in the dark and in the wet and in the cold, to save their houses and their livelihood, and then hunkered down to await the end of the rain-lashed night.

Inside the Arguelles house, everyone was oblivious to this other, lower, more pedestrian aspect of the life of Camarines. They were able to ignore the difficulties brought about by the typhoon because they had an army of servants that dealt with the worst of it. Margarita took one last survey of the place before the first of the guests arrived, and was once more gratified at her handiwork. It was a small blessing that the electricity was still on, the electric lines probably holding on to their posts with much more force than expected, so the ballroom was truly a sight to behold. Still the threat of a power interruption continued to bother her, but for now, the Arguelleses and their house were ready.

At exactly six o'clock in the evening, Jacobo and Margarita were already standing in place by the huge main double doors, with Luningning and Toriano, one of the more senior of the menservants. Outside, bearing large black umbrellas, were several men who worked for the house—two gardeners, three of the guards, two errand boys, and one of the men from the stables. A block of cement was temporarily placed, from where the motor cars would park, and led up to the set of señorita steps, which was thankfully already roofed in cement and plaster since the house was first built. The block of cement was raised six inches from the ground, and was covered with a rubberized tarpaulin, so the guests would not get mud on their shoes. A wide awning was set up over the cement block so the guests would get the least amount of rainfall on themselves.

At about eight minutes past six, in came Sofia, Marta, and Silvestre Monsantillo with their parents, Salvador and Consuela. The men shook hands amiably and asked about each other's haciendas. The women sniffed each other's cheeks, left and right, and then the Monsantillos were promptly ushered into the ballroom. The next to arrive were a quartet of old female Visbales: Carmelita Visbal, Delilah Visbal, Amparo Visbal-Visbal, and Imelda Visbal viuda de Visbal. They were welcomed by Jacobo and Margarita, who thought they looked perfectly at ease in such disturbing weather, with their long, slim dresses, kohl-lined eyes and jewellery that looked much heavier than themselves, that Margarita thought they could all topple over on to the carpet any time, as they walked slowly, as if in a trance, to the ballroom.

Next came the Governor of Camarines, and then the Archbishop with his favourite parish priest. The Chief of the Constabulary also arrived with his wife, as well as some of the business partners of Jacobo with their wives. Then three different members of the House of Representatives arrived, their wives clinging to their arms. The mayors of the many towns covered by the haciendas also arrived. The wave of guests, all dressed in finery and bedecked with jewels, was eager to see who was wearing what, whispering to each other their judgements about who looked older than she actually was, and which young man was next going to woo which young woman—usual gossip in a family that had made it a habit to intermarry and thus end up sharing and inheriting not just blood but histories and land and power and ancestral habits and misconduct.

By half past six, the ballroom has become a decorous cacophony. Jacobo and Margarita mingled with the guests, Jacobo being, with much effort, uncharacteristically smiling and more talkative than usual, and Margarita being just as uncharacteristically kind, appreciative, welcoming and very convivial. Mercedes did not feel it necessary to adjust her own personality for the event. She quietly sat on a wingback chair near the largest window of the room, observing everyone else, and even beyond the tightly shut windows and the closed drapes, she could hear the sounds that were heralding the voice that was going to call her name soon.

At seven o'clock, on the dot, Esperanza's moment came. Jacobo and Margarita walked to the closed doors of the ballroom, had the double doors opened to reveal the grand stairway that led from the foyer to the upstairs part of the house, and Margarita clapped her hands to get everyone's attention.

'Mira! Mira! My dear friends and allies, thank you all for coming to this event despite the terrible weather. By this time, we should know ourselves enough to understand that a tiny storm will not get in the way of a momentous occasion such as this.' A mild laughter went around the room, and a few of the guests cheered. 'Please gather around, *por favor*,' and the guests walked closer to the double doors.

Jacobo stepped up, and announced, 'May I now present my daughter, Esperanza Arguelles, on her eighteenth birthday?' and gestured to the grand stairway, bedecked with flowers and lit by warm, delicate lights.

Esperanza, at the top landing, took her moment, smiled down at everyone, and slowly began her descent, which she had actually practised many times before, often with Sofia, and with Margarita making sure she did the proper way of walking down the stairs.

Esperanza was a vision to behold, a spectacle of beauty, refinement, and such vibrant youth, her head bearing Esmeralda's tiara, which reflected the lights of the chandelier. Her dress looked lambent amid the lights that invisibly cascaded down the staircase, ingeniously placed by Margarita and her servants among the flowers and vines that twirled around the banisters and the posts. The shades of swirling pink of Esperanza's dress made her look like she was in a constant, slowly rotating motion, even as she walked down the stairs in the practised manner that her mother taught her.

Esperanza looked down at her guests gathered at the foyer, and smiled sincerely, pleased with herself, grateful to her mother, and in her head whirled all of her dreams all at once, in one seething eddy. All the while, Mercedes could see that Esperanza, the one with the most ambition and the most lofty of dreams, would end up the most cursed and bitter of them all. Her name, standing for 'hope', would retain its spirit of anticipation of better things in the future, but these will not be realized. The girl will turn into an old, bent woman eternally fuming at the world, her broken, shrunken, wrinkled body staying relentlessly alive even when her heart and soul would be begging for death. But tonight, Esperanza was the picture of a true Arguelles at the height of power, and Mercedes allowed her her night of glory.

As Esperanza approached the bottom landing, everyone held up their champagne glasses to cheer, and she stood between her father and her mother, near the double doors that led to the ballroom. Mercedes stood near the front of the crowd, beside two of the Visbal-Visbales, and in the warm, amber light, could barely make out the personage of Esmeralda, standing near the doors to the lanai that had been shut against the typhoon. The drapes were pinkish, and Esmeralda wore a dress of a very light colour, very similar to the colour of her skin, and she looked almost transparent. She was standing in a quarter profile, and Mercedes could see that the apparition wore absolutely no jewellery. She was also looking straight at Mercedes, who raised her glass to Esmeralda. At that moment, Esmeralda nodded ever so slightly and then dissolved into the drapes and the light. Mercedes's hand automatically went up to caress the huge butterfly necklace she was wearing, ready for what she knew was coming, and thankful that she would not be around to witness what would come after that.

But outside of Mercedes's thoughts and experience, Esperanza's debut went on. By this time, everyone had already entered through the double doors of the ballroom, where a long table was set with an elaborate dinner. Jacobo handed Esperanza her own champagne glass and proposed a toast, 'To my eldest daughter, Esperanza, hija, may you continue to have a life of bounty, and may you continue to have love around you. As you pursue your life, this time as an adult, may you never forget the traditions and the virtues of the family that we have come from.'

Jacobo stepped closer to Esperanza and kissed her squarely on the cheek. *'Feliz cumpleano, mi hija. Te quiero mucho.'*

Margarita raised her glass and announced, 'To my beautiful, beloved daughter, may you have the freedom to live the life the way you want to, without forgoing the virtues that make you who you truly are,' and then she also kissed Esperanza on her other cheek. *'Te amo, hija.'*

And then everyone, including Mercedes, raised their glasses again and drank to Esperanza's good fortune. Mercedes did try to be happy for her granddaughter, if only for this night. Indeed, this was not a night to ponder about bleak futures. Despite the typhoon raging darkly outside, this was still a night to bask in the glory of a golden age that everyone thought would never end, even as stories of a possible uprising in the haciendas can no longer be lightly dismissed.

Inside the ballroom, the typhoon that threw Esperanza into histrionics the day before had been all but forgotten by the bejewelled star of the show. Her female friends and cousins clustered around her to praise her on how good she looked, and several young men, some of them Jacobo II's classmates from the seminario and some of them Monsantillos and the more normal-looking Visbales, focused their attention on the debutante. They took their turns trying to get her to walk with them to a quieter area of the ballroom so they could talk to her with a little more privacy. Esperanza flirted with all of them, of course, but then her eyes fell on Silvestre Monstantillo, who she had not seen for an entire year, and she instantly fell in love. He looked taller, and his shoulders were broader, and she felt like he had grown more hair. She also thought that his voice had gotten louder, and he had grown more confident, smiled more, and altogether had grown to be a little more than what he used to be. He was still Silvestre, but more handsome and dashing than the Silvestre from last year, and Esperanza, enthralled, now focused her attention on him.

Unable to flip her hair because it was up in a chignon to accommodate Esmeralda's tiara, she instead fluttered her dainty, embroidered handkerchief, which matched her dress, at some silly joke a male friend told her, and then covered her mouth shyly to smile, while overtly batting her heavily mascaraed eyelashes at Silvestre, who was looking at her and taking it all in.

All this time the string quartet, composed of female music teachers from the Colegio de Santa Rita, had been playing various waltzes. Esperanza's official first dance was with her father and then with Jacobo II and then with a series of men that had been pre-selected into a particular order by Margarita, according to their closeness to the Arguelleses and according to their status in society. By some fate, Margarita decided that Esperanza's final dance would be with Silvestre before the dance was declared open for all.

When it was Silvestre's turn, he held out his hand to Esperanza and said, 'May I please have this dance?' Though she knew this was part of the programme, and that his manner was completely customary, Esperanza's heart still gave a little jump. She placed her hand in his, and they danced the waltz, just the two of them, in the centre of the ballroom, with everyone else silently looking on.

'Thank you for coming,' Esperanza said, putting on her best smile that she had practised many times in her room before this moment.

'You look very beautiful,' Silvestre replied, and he meant it. A year ago, she was all hair and dress and drama, and not much face, but now she was a true vision. She had lost a little of her chubbiness, and her hair, corralled in her chignon, made her appear more mature, which, to Silvestre, meant she probably carried less drama now.

Just then, while Silvestre and Esperanza had not even wrapped up their waltz, there were some loud thuds heard from outside of the main door. This puzzled Luningning, who was standing outside the ballroom. She looked quizzically at Toriano who was left guarding the door, because no other guests were expected at this hour. Toriano opened one door slightly and then suddenly fell back as he saw who was standing outside.

It was a man, a huge, dark, hulking man, a man they had never seen before and who was thus not part of the household, his hair longish and dripping wet in the rain. The man stood there on the top landing of the señorita steps, his face lighted by the large sconces on either side of the double doors. He had a bolo in his hand.

Luningning and Toriano were transfixed, unable to move or speak. The man lunged forward briskly, trailing water, and ran the direction of the ballroom whose doors were fully open.

Luningning cried, 'Stop!' and Toriano, after several seconds, began running after the man, but he was already inside the ballroom, and it was too late.

'Don Jacobo!' the man roared. At once everyone stopped eating, drinking, talking, dancing, playing music, to look at the spectacle by the door. Toriano grabbed the man's waist from behind, but the man shook him off. From inside the ballroom someone screamed, which incited others to do the same. Assumpta, who had been standing in a corner of the foyer for a few minutes, having been able to escape the soirée because she was planning to go to her secret room to read in the bathtub, saw Tiyong Pato, the head guard, rush in with several of the house's guards.

Inside the ballroom, Jacobo, who was at the back of the room with Jacobo II, talking to the Archbishop, strode towards the door to face the man, but Pato and his men got to him first, pinned him to the ground and carried him away. A very flustered Luningning ran into the ballroom and, with the help of Toriano, who had managed to compose himself quickly, they closed the double doors of the ballroom, instinctively to protect their masters but also effectively sealing all of the well-appointed people inside. Mercedes and Margarita looked at each other across the room, because each knew how the other felt. And in each other's eyes they saw, simultaneously, that they both recalled their feelings of doom when they first stepped in through the threshold of their house, each in their own time in history, but both felt, in unison, that this could be what their feeling of predestined ruination meant and that it was about to begin.

Chapter 7

Letters

The spectacle from the night before was the topic of conversation for everyone in all the three haciendas and most of Camarines, for the next several days. As the story was passed on from mouth to mouth, there were of course many additions and subtractions inadvertently made to the details, until what emerged was that during Esperanza's debut celebration in the house at Hacienda Marianita, three large, hulking men carrying bolos and dripping from the storm barged through the windows of the ballroom, declared a revolution, and had to be shot down by the Chief of Police and his deputies right in the middle of the dinner. Jacobo II was wounded in the knee by a stray bullet while the string quartet played Tchaikovsky, and one of the several Visbales suffered a heart attack and had to be rushed to the hospital amid the storm. The motor car that was driving her almost met with an accident on the flooded and slippery asphalt road to the hospital in the middle of the town, which worsened her condition and almost killed her, but she was admitted to the hospital in time and her life was saved.

And then the inevitable prophecies followed closely. The events of the night before supposedly meant that Esperanza was doomed to a life of social disgrace, that Hacienda Marianita would be overrun with many more of these men, who were actually members of a breakaway Hukbalahap group that were never caught before because they had gone into hiding for a decade until they found it appropriate to regroup and wreak havoc again, and that the other two families' fate would follow suit with that of the Arguelleses.

Nothing in that story was true. There was only one man and no one had had a heart attack, and the Hukbalahap had nothing to do with anything. The only part of the gossip that was true was that the Chief of Police was indeed present at the debut as a guest, although without his deputy, and that, more importantly, the three families' fates were inextricably linked. This fact the servants and the other rumours simply glossed over but little did they know that this was the truest of all the details of the convoluted and transmogrified stories they passed on to each other.

But here, exactly, is what had actually happened. After the doors to the ballroom were closed by Luningning and Toriano, and Jacobo slipped out through a side door with Jacobo II, Salvador Monstantillo, and the Chief of Police, one of Tiyong Pato's guards ran back into the foyer to say that the man had escaped. Jacobo ordered the guards to search the entire premises, beginning with the area surrounding the house, and to find the man and bring him to Tiyong Pato's headquarters near the house.

The guards searched in the storm for about an hour, using bicycles and motorcycles and horses, later on expanding their search to the farther reaches of the house grounds, and yet the man, whom no one could identify even though they had seen his face squarely for several minutes in the bright ballroom, had not been found. Jacobo returned to the soirée, while several guards stayed close to the house and regularly roved the grounds for the safety of the people inside. Tiyong Pato eventually returned to confirm that they found no one in the area covering about seven kilometres from the house. The Chief of Police then told Jacobo to see him in his office in the town centre the next morning with the witnesses.

Back inside the ballroom, in the soirée, Margarita managed to convince the teenagers to dance to a more lively tune that she asked the string quartet to play, in an effort to distract everyone from what had just happened. Esperanza, still in the arms of Silvestre, remained stunned the longest, in the middle of the dance floor. Margarita, Silvestre and Sofia had to gently lead her to a settee at the back of the ballroom, away from everyone else. The string quartet played, the teenagers danced, the servants brought in more food and wine, and after a while, people started laughing again, mostly because they were content knowing that this was an Arguelles problem, not theirs, and it was because of this that the soirée unexpectedly outlasted the storm. The soirée wrapped up a little before three o'clock in the morning. An hour before that, the rain had slowed down to a slow drizzle. Assumpta, Paz, Guadalupe and Inez have been sent to bed at around ten o'clock, with Mrs Palacio drowsily tucking the youngest ones into bed. The older guests began leaving at half past midnight, but the younger guests stayed to continue the dancing and the parent-sanctioned drinking. Esperanza, now drunk after deciding to drink away her growing sense of social destruction, appeared like a bacchanalian princess in a tiara and swirls of pink fabric, and because of what happened at her very own birthday soirée, she was allowed her night of debauchery, with Luningning and a few remaining servants standing guard near her to keep her in check just in case she got into a more uncontrollable inebriated frenzy.

Esperanza was being very flirtatious with Silvestre Monsantillo, who was soon to graduate with a college degree under a double major from the Ateneo de Naga. Talks had been going around that his father might allow him to travel to some countries for a while first, see the world, before settling permanently at Hacienda Vida. He was a rather tall fellow, like a Visbal, but had the robust and athletic look and built of a Monsantillo. Esperanza's flirting was not lost on him, and he reciprocated. They walked out to the inner courtyard, took the limestone steps to prevent their shoes from getting wet, and stayed outside to whisper between themselves and laugh and flirt, right near the others but a little farther away. Luckily, they were standing underneath the sealed rooms of Marianita, so no one could hear exactly what they were talking about, but everyone who remained in the soirée could see them, including the watch guard Luningning, and she duly took note of the situation.

Mercedes, on the other hand, had retired to her room at past midnight. She sat at her dresser, made of carved mahogany with mother-of-pearl inlays, which she had inherited from her mother-in-law, and looked at her herself silently in the mirror, still wearing Esmeralda's pearls. She took a while doing this, thinking, still wondering, despite her rather strong convictions, what Esmeralda's appearance could have meant. Could she, Mercedes, be dying? Or would she be told yet another secret, deeper and more hideous than the secrets she had already been carrying for most of her life? Who else did Esmeralda show herself to? Not the servants, certainly, or else there would have already been an outbreak downstairs in the servants' quarters. She wasn't that close to Margarita to ask her if she also saw Esmeralda. So this was yet another secret that Mercedes decided that she had to keep, pending the final realization of her very first and most indisputable feeling that she would die soon. This, and that disturbance during the soirée, made her believe that Esperanza's debut was the mark of some decline.

She took off Esmeralda's jewellery, slowly and ceremoniously, kissed each piece before she laid them on their velvet resting places, and sat a little bit more at her dresser looking at herself, at her wrinkled face, which was made up for the occasion, and looked around her room through the three-panelled mirror of her dresser, half expecting to see Esmeralda again. But Esmeralda had appeared to Mercedes for the very last time earlier that night at the *lanai*, and Mercedes would never see her again. Instead, Mercedes began to hear the chains, very faintly rattling through the walls.

Then the sound of the heavy load followed, and then the slow, shuffling footsteps of a being that had been walking with a great weight for so many generations. It was the *multong condenado*, reminding her of her guilt of omission, but Mercedes could no longer feel any dread in her heart at the company of the ghost. She knew that she would be spared from witnessing the disasters that were to come. She washed up, dressed down for bed, and sat up under her damask sheets, propped up by her pillows, and prayed to La Virgen de Guadalupe by the light of one bedside lamp, though she didn't need the light, as she had already memorized the entire novena through the years.

Margarita, alone in her bed as usual, sleepless because of what had just happened that evening, suspected that Jacobo and the entire hacienda was most probably already in the throes of a deep problem that he had told her nothing about. Yet she worried not for Jacobo, but for her children. When most of the grownups had gone home, Margarita called Luningning and asked her what she had heard, and she was told that the man had escaped. At this, Margarita remembered, for the second time that night, that same sense of strange foreboding that she felt upon crossing the threshold of the Arguelles house for the very first time, and which she felt again during the spectacle that evening.

It was a measure of how far apart she had grown from her husband of a quarter of a century, when her sense of foreboding made her focus mostly on her children rather than on the man who was tasked to save the hacienda—and their entire family—from an incoming struggle, and who of course needed her support. She tossed and turned in bed, got thirsty, and got out of bed to get a glass of water from the carafe she always kept on the bedside table. Then she saw him again, the tall, thin, multong fantasma, his white, almost luminous shirt pristine as ever, standing by the door to her bathroom, looking at her, judging her, accusing her of doing nothing of importance regarding the concerns at hand.

Margarita did not feel afraid. In fact, she waited for the ghost to say something, anything, that would give her a clue as to how to proceed. How could she go back to Jacobo, to rekindle their marriage, which had already survived so much, she with her pride and her scruples? How could she protect her children? How could she help protect the hacienda that had been strong and standing for the better part of two hundred years? She stood there, facing the ghost, who likewise stood right where he was and looked back at her, as still as a statue, saying nothing. And then, slowly, his image disappeared into the wall, and Margarita was left looking at nothing.

Mercedes and Margarita were not the only ones sleepless that night. Jacobo, of course, the one most intensely and directly involved in it all, could not even get into his bed. He dragged his chair to the window, opened up the drapes and the window panes and shutters to the cold and still-drizzling weather outside, while keeping all of his lights closed. He looked out into his gardens, his trees, his fields, his hills, while holding yet another glass of bourbon. He was still wearing his white tie, complete with the shoes, and there he sat on his chair, by the window, paralyzed. The glass of bourbon in his hand stayed unmoved on top of his knee, while his mind wandered through all the decisions he had made in the past.

From as far back as Jacobo could possibly remember, even before he took over the management of the hacienda from his older brother, who had developed an illness that prevented him from working for the hacienda full time, Jacobo and all of his brothers had been indoctrinated by their father, Alfonso, that the hacienda comes before all else and that their only collective purpose in life now was to nurture, empower, and protect what the family had done and had been doing for a very long time. In Jacobo's own time, when he began managing the hacienda, he had tried to be as fair as possible in every business dealing, except when the business dealing became a threat to the life and health of the hacienda. He felt that he had been kind and generous to all his good and honest workers, but ruthless with those ones who weren't. He never felt he needed to project the image of stern and merciless Spanish hidalgo, but over the years, at times, Jacobo had needed to be harsh, even brutal, but only for the good of the hacienda, and he battled with his conscience so that he would eventually see no fault in what he had done. For the Arguelleses, God and the hacienda were one, the latter existing because of the former, and so it was not only their mission but their birthright and the destiny of their bloodline.

Jacobo remembered several old business deals that had gone sour and caused the loss of certain business partners. He also remembered that famously failed bargain with one of the former Governors of Camarines, in which the Governor proposed a sort of trade and in which Jacobo would give the titles to some of Hacienda Marianita's properties to the Governor while the Governor, in return, would try to manipulate the farm gate prices for all produce coming from Hacienda Marianita. Jacobo, his silence and introspection belying a shrewd and exceptional skill at seeing through the real purpose of the business proposals of all his associates, said no to the scheme right away, and the Governor walked out of the house in a huff. That very night, about ten full hectares of corn in one of Hacienda Marianita's areas, ready for harvest in about a week or so, were set ablaze. Jacobo, acting true to the fierce blood of the Arguelles, plotted to have the Governor shot. Jacobo set up a drunken man, who owed a lot to Jacobo, to be the fall guy, and he was thus arrested, and after a week committed suicide inside his jail cell. This allowed the Arguelleses impunity, and that was the end of the entire matter. The Vice-Governor took over as interim Governor until the next elections, and since then, no one from the provincial capitol ever approached Jacobo for any business dealings at all. If anything, any associations they maintained since then had always been social, and men of weaker constitution and vacillating ambitions tended to steer clear of Jacobo.

Then there was the case of the woman, a daughter of one of the hacienda's farmers, that Caruso, Jacobo's older brother by about four years, had a sort of love affair with, leading to the woman's pregnancy. Caruso had always been known to be a ladies' man, and in fact, he chose to travel the world instead of staying in Camarines to help manage the hacienda. He must have had love affairs with so many women in so many countries, and Jacobo was relieved that they were living in other countries or one day he would be beset with an army of young ladies carrying babies that they would claim was Caruso's. Caruso never married, and he didn't want to have anything to do with the farm girl after that and fled to Paris. Jacobo, of course, didn't want any stray Arguelles blood diluting the bloodline, so he arranged for her instant disposal. One morning she was found drowned in the irrigation levee, and the incident was ruled an accident.

There were many more before and after that, people who tried to get one over Jacobo, because Hacienda Marianita at the time was the most bountiful, most efficiently managed, with the most loyal workers, and most secure of all three haciendas in Camarines. But there were also people who sincerely just made honest mistakes, or were themselves wronged by the Arguelleses to begin with, but Jacobo treated them the same way he did the scheming ones. Indeed, it paid to be a close business partner of Jacobo, but it often came at a cost. The man that Margarita simply nagged and then ignored, and then eventually dismissed, happened to be the most dangerous man in the province. That was how little the husband and wife knew about each other.

So Jacobo sat by the window in his bedroom, all the while listening to the faint strains of laughter and music that came from the still-ongoing soirée at the ballroom. By now, because the rains had already all but stopped, the windows and the lanai doors would already have been opened, and the young ladies and gentlemen would have been enjoying the new damp coolness after the rather stuffy atmosphere earlier. Jacobo sighed, rubbed his signet ring, which had been on his finger since Christmas of 1948, and finally decided to drink his bourbon. As he was slowly lifting the glass to his mouth, a rather strong force knocked the glass out of his hand and into the opposite wall. The glass shattered, and Jacobo was stunned for just a very brief moment. Then he stood up from his chair, reached for the nearest lamp and pulled the cord to turn on the light, and saw, from the opposite corner of his bedroom, a woman dressed in black and with indescribable wrath in her eyes. She was a little bit hunched over, and she was breathing heavily, her shoulders moving up and down in a belaboured manner, and Jacobo could actually hear her wheezing. Her hands clenched into fists. She was fair-skinned, and looked rather familiar to Jacobo, but he could not quite place her.

But of course the most dangerous man in the province would not fall faint at the sight and tantrums of what Jacobo now recognized as a multong vengativa, so he asked her, in his full voice, 'What do you want?'

She didn't answer, but simply glared at him with all the fury in her eyes. Then she unclenched one fist and slowly pointed a finger straight at Jacobo, and then disappeared.

Whereas the other two women, Arguelleses only by name, did not feel that doom in their own blood but only in their hearts, from time to time, by association, Jacobo had carried that feeling of doom in the weight of his blood for all of his life. And that was why, on that night, he decided the he would do everything that he could, defy everything that he possibly could and should, so that Hacienda Marianita would not fall for at least another two hundred years, and continue to be rich and powerful long beyond that. However, his vision of the hacienda's future was not the same as the hacienda's destiny. On the very early morning after Esperanza turned eighteen, Hacienda Marianita began its secret rending.

With very little sleep, Mercedes emerged from her room fully dressed, carrying Esmeralda's pearls and the other jewellery in their special cases, prepared to be driven to the bank to place them all back into the safe deposit boxes. The other jewellery sets were collected early that morning by Luningning. Margarita was also awake early, and she had the jewellery ready in their cases when Luningning came by to take them, but Esperanza was still asleep in her bedroom under a mound of pillows, her hair half out of the chignon, and still wearing the rest of the jewellery, although the diamond tiara was tossed carelessly on top of a side table. Margarita had to dig through the layers of pillows and taffeta and organza and chiffon before she could get to Esperanza, who was reeking of drunkenness, to take off the jewellery, put them back into their special cases, and hand them to Luningning, who then gave them all to Mercedes.

In the town of Toog, people were in the middle of fixing, restoring, rebuilding what Typhoon Luisa had destroyed the night before. Many a sheet of corrugated metal had been torn off their frames from atop shops and offices and houses. Glass window panes, those that were not covered by cardboard or sheet metal scraps before the storm came, shattered, quite expectedly. Entire walls made of plywood were peeled off their frames, and, once the wind and rain had entered any building, everything that was inside was fair game, not just to the typhoon but also to scoundrels who took advantage of the storm to steal from whichever building was left unguarded. The houses that were made of nipa, their nipa roofs held in place by old discarded rubber tires, did not lose their roofs, but they were nevertheless beaten to the ground in their entirety, as if a giant mallet had pounded on them repeatedly from the side till the nipa huts were literally flat on the ground that the typhoon had also turned to mud, flat on the ground like the stalks of Jacobo's palay farms, everything inside the flattened nipa huts also flattened, their human and animal inhabitants usually taking shelter in whatever large tree was left standing nearby. These nipa huts would be taken apart, the pieces sorted through, the broken parts repaired, and then a new nipa hut would be rebuilt using the salvaged and the repaired pieces, while the missing pieces would be filled in as the days went by from scavenged items, parts donated by neighbours, and some ayuda given by the town mayor, other local politicians, the parish priest, and Jacobo.

Not all work could resume in the town centre of Toog the day after Typhoon Luisa, for the day had to be devoted to rebuilding what had been torn down, which was most of Toog, a town whose economic and cultural life revolved around Hacienda Marianita. Jacobo was also out of the house very early with his chauffeur Elmer, to go to Ilawod to meet Apolonio, his encargado in the palay farm there. The morning before Typhoon Luisa arrived, the stalks of the palay had already been bent to the ground, as Sebastian many, many years ago had taught his workers and encargados and sons, and who, in turn, taught the men that came after them. However, they could do this only to the stalks that had not yet entered the panicle stage, when the actual grain of rice had not yet been created by the plant inside one of the nodes in its stalk. A rice stalk in this stage that is submerged in water for an entire night and pulled up straight again on the very next morning can still continue its life, proceed to germinate, flower, get fertilized, and then mature enough to be harvested. But stalks that were already pregnant with grains could not withstand being steeped in water, and would die. In Ilawod, about a fifth of Jacobo's palay farm had stalks that had already entered the panicle stage, so he had struck those out of his projected harvest even before the storm came. Another fifth was fallow land, but the rest were in different stages of growth and could be bent down. Apolonio, sleepless the night before because Filomena could not stay with him during the typhoon, spent the time waiting impatiently for the dawn to meet Jacobo, and watch the farm workers stream in to pull the stalks back upright again.

It was a quick visit. Jacobo walked along the dikes where the stalks were bent down, and he was especially pleased as he watched his workers methodically working. They stayed long enough to see that the work was going as planned, and then left to see the Chief of Police about the matter of the unidentified man that made a spectacle in his ballroom the night before. By the time Jacobo was stepping into the office of the Chief of Police in the town centre, Mercedes was also stepping into the bank with the jewellery that she was to place back inside the safe deposit box meant specially for them. But that day, she planned to take something else back with her from a different safety deposit box: the letters of Marianita Enojado Arguelles.

Assumpta also had important things to do the day after Esperanza's debut. While everyone was preoccupied with tasks, errands, gossip, worry, and the dismantling of everything that had been set up in the ballroom for the night before, she hauled her briefcase of hand-drawn maps, and now Sebastian's thin sheaf of papers, into her secret room, so she could go through them, update them, colour them, read them, in absolute peace. The almost-daily rains had been keeping Paz indoors all day lately, so Assumpta could not stay in her bedroom to do what she wanted to do, because she knew how Paz would just scoff at her and complain about her mess, and would sometimes even pretend to accidentally sit or step on some of her papers. So early that morning, after a big breakfast from which Esperanza, Jacobo, and Jacobo II were absent, as Jacobo II was also down with a hangover, Assumpta ran off before anyone could ask her where she was going, and then resolutely began her day.

She sat on the cold concrete floor and began spreading out Sebastian's papers in front of her. All in all, she counted fourteen pages. The writing on all of them were in a tall, spiky handwriting, very slanted and thin. The ink was brown in some places and grey in some places, but for the most part still readable, if she could figure out the words. Her Spanish was very rudimentary, but after much effort and squinting, she was able to make out some of the words. The other Spanish words looked too complicated with the unfamiliar handwriting, so she glossed over them, but she went over the pages again, and wrote down on a new piece of paper the words that she could make out. She could read abono, recompensa, perdicion, Alonzo, perdon, Lorenzo Monsantillo, amor, Pilita Arguelles, and salido. As she went over Sebastian's papers another time, she could make out even more words, and continued her list on her sheet of paper, taking her time to make her lines less shaky. Mrs Palacio would be pleased, Assumpta thought. While she was writing words on paper, ensconced in her secret concrete room with the claw-foot bathtub, Jacobo walked into the house at Hacienda Marianita, walked up the stairs to his office on the third floor, and began gathering the paperwork about the hacienda that he needed to hide. Around them, the wood and mortar of the house at Hacienda Marianita heaved very slightly, as if stirring from sleep, the ground below it also stirring. With the words on Sebastian's papers and Jacobo's actions, something was being roused, slowly, through deep time.

Chapter 8

Wounds of the Land

While the Arguelleses continued to deal with their ancestral ghosts brought about by their ancestral guilt, about two months after Esperanza's debut, the Monsantillos began to experience a more immediate and practical problem. Their palay farms in Mangkono, all of twenty-six hectares, had developed some kind of disease. Even amid close and efficient care, the palay farms of Hacienda Vida had developed a disease called tungro, which rots the part of the stalk that was underground and lessens the growth of the plant's stalk leaves. The surviving stalks, though they would eventually grow to maturity as scheduled, would nevertheless produce hollow and empty seeds. As if that were not enough, as if on cue, the paddies were overrun by small pink snails, which feed on whatever stalks that end up growing despite the tungro. Salvador Monsantillo was plunged into despair. Hacienda Vida's palay harvests made up about 40 per cent of his total produce, and now an entire palay season would go to waste because of the infestation and the disease.

He quickly summoned his encargados from the palay farms and two of his three administrators, and they all tried to save the situation. His encargados were tasked to find a cure, or perhaps just an inhibiting factor for the tungro, and to vanquish, to some degree, the pink snails and their effects. The administrators were made to figure out just how much damage the hacienda would have to suffer through for this planting season, and to strategize how to survive the season financially despite this certain loss.

They also looked at Salvador's other enterprises, to see which could be used to help save the grim financial situation that the blight would cause. They went through the list of names of their business partners, sought out the ones that used to offer the highest price for the hacienda's seasonal produce of abaca, sugarcane and tilapia. The fruit and vegetable plantations were far too small to be of any help, so they just let that be. On the other hand, abaca was Salvador's second-largest source of income, so they checked their production for this season and went to the plantations, factories and warehouses to inspect their progress and condition.

The nineteen-hectare abaca plantation seemed to be doing as well as it normally did. Salvador talked to his encargado Manuel and his head farmer at the plantation, who guided him and his administrators around the carefully planted stalks, laid out in a specific grid. Five hectares of the plantation would be ready for harvest in a year, while the other three quarters would be ready in two, three, and four years, respectively. Salvador felt immensely relieved at this, praised Manuel for his good work, and, though abaca as a plant did not really have any history of special diseases or infestations, warned him to be vigilant nonetheless. Then Salvador, his administrators, and Manuel left for the town to inspect the abaca warehouses and processing plants, fervently praying that nothing would be amiss there.

The processing plants turned out to be doing normally, causing Salvador to feel another sense of relief, this time with the conviction that not all was lost, and the problem would persist only with the palay farm and only this harvest season. But that was before they got to the first warehouse, the largest of them, which held more than half of his abaca stocks. The very moment they stepped into that warehouse, Salvador could distinctly smell the strong musty odour of moisture, a condition deadly for abaca fibers, which should always be kept dry and within a particular range of temperature. Immediately, Jacobo looked at the ageing warehouseman, who was the one who let them in, and asked, 'Do you smell that?'

'Smell what, Don Salvador?'

'That smell! The wet smell!'

'I don't smell any wet smell, Don Salvador.'

This infuriated Salvador at once, and he shouted, 'You cannot smell that? I can smell that a kilometre away!'

'Pardon, Don Salvador, but I don't smell anything strange. The hemp is in normal conditions.'

'Well, have you been measuring temperature and humidity factors every day?'

'Yes, of course, Don Salvador.'

'But I can smell the dampness in here!' bawled out Salvador. He turned to one of his administrators, and asked him, 'Do you smell that?'

'Definitely, Don Salvador.'

Salvador asked the other administrator, ' How about you?'

'I do smell something moldy.'

'*Madre de Dios!*' Salvador roared out. 'Something is very wrong here!' Then he turned to the warehouseman and pointed a finger at him, 'You. Give me the daily logs of the measurement readings.'

The warehouseman, stooped with age and trembling with fear, went to fetch the logbook from his table, and handed it to Salvador deferentially, with shuddering hands. Salvador wrenched the logbook from the warehouseman and flipped through to the latest readings, covering the past week. All seemed within normal ranges, indeed. Humidity and temperature were held in check, almost clinically so, because there were almost no variations, even though Camarines had been experiencing the usual August rain-and-shine cycle. There must have been changes in humidity and temperature inside the warehouse, which would require the adjustment of the settings of the humidifiers and the temperature controls built inside the warehouse, but the logbook showed no such fluctuations in the readings, and therefore, no changes were made to the regulators.

Salvador saw that for the past week, all readings were exactly the same. For the two weeks before that, all numbers were the same as well, which was impossible for a climate such as that of Camarines. Still clutching the logbook, he strode over to the temperatures and humidifiers. He knelt before them, placed his ear against them, and knocked on various places of the equipment. And then he stood up and flung the logbook at the equipment.

'Inutil!' Salvador roared. 'The instruments are not working! That's why for the past three weeks you have not been seeing any changes to the readings!'

'They are not working, Don Salvador?' echoed the warehouseman, now visibly trembling from where he was standing.

'That's exactly what I said! Did you not figure that out, you *tonto*? Did you not find it strange that there have been no changes to the readings for three whole weeks? How long have you been working here?

'Th- th- thirty-seven years, Don Salvador,' the warehouseman stammered.

'And in those thirty-seven years, did it ever happen before that for three weeks the temperatures and the humidity levels in this warehouse have not changed?'

'N-no, Do- Don Salvador.' The warehouseman hung his head in defeat.

'Then did you not suspect anything when you started to smell the wetness in here?'

'D- D- Don Salvador, I d- do not smell anything.'

'But we all do!' Salvador gestured towards his two administrators, who nodded fiercely. Then he looked pointedly at Manuel, who had already turned pale several minutes ago, when Salvador started becoming irate.

'D- D- Don Salvador, what I me- mean is that I can-cannot smell anything,' said the warehouseman in a weak and trembling voice. 'I have b- been s- s- sick, and I have had a c-cold, and I could not smell anything.'

'What? *Estupido*! Then why have you been coming to work if you are sick?'

'Because I feel strong enough to work, Don Salvador.'

'Yes, but both your nose and your mind are not. Tonto! Inutil!'

'Pardon, Don Salvador,' said the warehouseman, for lack of anything more to say.

'And you!' said Salvador, turning to Manuel. 'Have you never checked here, all three weeks?'

'My wife has been sick, Don Salvador, I barely had the time,' Manuel replied weakly.

'*Dios mio!* Everyone has a reason!'

Salvador took off his eyeglasses and pinched the bridge of his nose. He was starting to have a migraine, and just wanted to go home, but he had to deal with things in order to prevent his ruin. On the other hand, it was almost high noon, and he needed some rest, and time alone to think up a strategy.

'You two,' Salvador said, pointing at Manuel and then the warehouseman, 'you no longer work for me. I will give you the wages that you have earned this month, except for the wages for the past three weeks in which you have not done your duties. I am evicting your entire families from the house I allowed you to live in. You have three days to move out.'

Then he turned to one of his administrators. 'Make sure they are out in three days.'

Then to the other one, he said, 'Round up about seven men from the factories. Make them come here to turn this entire place over, and find out exactly where the wetness is, fix the whole area up, and have mechanics in here to fix these useless equipment.' Then he went over to one of the humidifiers and kicked it with his foot. 'Inutil!' He mumbled once again under his breath.

'I am going home,' Salvador told his administrators. 'You two deal with this right away, and report to me in the house at three o'clock this afternoon.'

The two administrators nodded, and Salvador walked out to his waiting motor car and told his chauffeur to take him home. He had no appetite for his usual full lunch, but he would like some suman and a cold drink, and try to have an hour's siesta, if his mind could calm down enough for that.

But there was no rest to be had in his own house. When he arrived, he heard his wife, Consuela, having an argument with Silvestre about Esperanza.

'I do not approve of her, hijo,' Consuela was saying. 'She is too modern for you.'

'Mama, I find that insulting,' Silvestre replied. 'Are you saying that only out-of-date *provincianas* are meant for me?'

'Of course I didn't mean that. I was referring to someone more in tune with hacienda life than someone who believes she belongs in Hollywood films,' said Consuela sarcastically.

'She is nothing like that!' Silvestre sounded annoyed.

'Oh, hijo. You might have already been blinded.'

'I am not blind, Mama. What do you take me for?'

'I just think she is not appropriate for life here, with you, in the hacienda,' Consuela, wanting to win, switched from sarcasm to what she hoped sounded like compassion to her son.

'How can that be when she has grown up and lived in a hacienda as well?'

'She might have lived all her live in a hacienda, but her mind is elsewhere. She is not meant for here,' Consuela explained, her tone now pleading. 'And then where would you be when she leaves?'

'Mama, sometimes you over-analyze things,' said Silvestre curtly, his brow furrowed and his lips pursed.

'I do not. I can see things you do not because I am also a woman.'

'Now we're going into the battle of the sexes.'

'Don't be sarcastic with me, Silvestre,' Consuela snapped.

Silvestre hung his head and then was about to say something when Consuela saw Salvador on his way to their bedroom.

'Tell him, Salvador,' said Consuela.

'Tell him what?' said Salvador wearily.

'About Esperanza.'

'What about Esperanza?' asked Salvador, still walking in the direction of his bedroom, hoping to somehow get out of the conversation.

'That she is not for him.'

'I have no time for that now.' And then Salvador turned, looked at Silvestre directly, and said, 'But I am telling you this. Do not make decisions when you are young. See the world first. Only then can you decide what you want and who you want,' and then he went upstairs.

'*Querido*, are you not going to have lunch?' Consuela called out after him.

'No. I'm tired. Go on without me,' he replied, then disappeared into the turn on the second landing.

Salvador was wearier than he had ever felt in his entire life, and then he remembered that with this blight in his produce, he might not even be able to spend for Silvestre's one year of travel overseas. His headache worsened, and he lost whatever was left of his appetite. He asked a servant for a large carafe of very cold drinking water and a glass, to shut the drapes in his room, and to wake him up at exactly three o'clock in the afternoon. He took off his over vest and his shirt and shoes, and slipped down his trousers, leaving on just his calzoncillos. When the water arrived, he quickly drank more than half of it, as if he had been lost in a dry and hot desert for days on end, and then fell to back to his pillows, asleep before his head even touched the embroidered silk. And while he slept, it rained.

Silvestre, under cover of the same rain and the siesta that everyone else was taking inside the house, slipped out via the halls of the servants' quarters, who were themselves having their own siesta, and out the utility door. He looked carefully around for the men that guarded the property, and saw no one. They were probably taking shelter from the typhoon. The security of the house at Hacienda Vida was also heightened after the appearance of the man with the bolo at the Arguelleses's, but now, two months after the incident, when nothing of a similar nature happened again, it seemed that the guards were starting to slacken.

Silvestre, in a long raincoat and rubber boots, walked stealthily to the garage to take his motorcycle. He pushed the vehicle through the mud and wet grass towards the gate, so that no one from the house could hear that he was leaving, and then when he was about half a kilometre from the house, his face completely drenched in rainwater, he started the motorcycle and set out from Hacienda Vida. The gatekeeper rushed to open one of the double gates, just enough to let the motorcycle through, and then Silvestre accelerated on the empty asphalt highway towards his pre-arranged meeting place with Esperanza. They agreed to meet at one of the small unused storage sheds that belonged to Salvador. It stood beside a rice processing plant because it used to house a generator set that powered the plant in case the town's electricity had problems. The Monsantillos had since upgraded to a larger generator set, which no longer fit that small storage shed, so the place remained more or less empty.

Five minutes after Silvestre arrived, there was a knock on the door; then it opened, and Esperanza walked in. She was also wearing a raincoat, and her hair under the hood was wrapped in a scarf.

'Did your driver suspect anything?' Silvestre asked.

'Not at all. He dropped me off at the bakery, and I told him to pick me up at the fabric store in two hours.'

'So we have two hours,' said Silvestre, walking closer to her.

'There could be snakes in here, you know,' Esperanza said, giggling.

Silvestre took her arm and pulled her even closer. 'I don't think so. Since when did you become scared of snakes?' he joked.

Esperanza giggled even more, shaking off the hood of her own raincoat, taking off the scarf, and smoothing down her long, curly hair. The two had met there twice already, to talk and neck and make plans for running away to America.

Just then, a woman's voice shouted from one of the dark corners of the storage shed. 'Who's there?' the voice called out.

The two lovers were startled. Silvestre took Esperanza's hand and pulled her to stand behind him.

'Who's there yourself!' He called out towards the direction of the voice. 'You are not supposed to be here.' He was not afraid. His father owned this place, and whoever it was who owned the voice was a trespasser.

'And neither are you,' answered the voice.

'Who are you? Show yourself,' Silvestre challenged.

'Ah, so you do not know about me then,' said the voice. And then they heard footsteps, and out into the half-light came a tall, striking-looking woman on the top landing.

'I am the "Oracle of Life and Death",' she declared, and waved her arms over her head.

Silvestre looked at Esperanza behind him and wryly said, 'It's just the town idiot.' Esperanza laughed, stepping away from behind Silvestre.

And then the Oracle of Life and Death, also known as the town idiot, began to dance around, waving her hands over her head quite gracefully. Her shawl seemed to float around her body and then over her head, mingling with her long, wavy hair. And then she began to laugh, wonderful and throaty.

'I see destruction! I see ruin! I see the hills falling back into the earth and the flatlands rising up to become hills, mountains! Sinkholes appearing in the plains to become oceans!'

Silvestre spoke up, 'And when, exactly, is this going to happen, O Wise Oracle?'

'Sooner than you think!' the woman laughed. 'Sooner than you think.'

'Well, since you are the Oracle, who therefore knows everything, could you at least give us a specific date?' Esperanza piped in, quite enjoying the revelation of the so-called prophecy.

'You challenge me, young lady? I will give you a day. It has begun two weeks ago, and will culminate in just a few months. When three families collide in wrath and deceit as Destiny requires, all of that will happen, and this world and its people will no longer be the same.' And the woman continued to dance and laugh.

Silvestre and Esperanza laughed with the village idiot. 'Let's get out of here,' Silvestre said, grabbing their raincoats and pulling Esperanza out through the door.

'Agreed,' said Esperanza, laughing. And, clad in their raincoats, they both got on the motorcycle under the pouring rain, Esperanza tightly gripping Silvestre's waist, and then they drove off. A paperback copy of Peyton Place peeked out from the pocket of Esperanza's raincoat, and its pages started to get wet at the edges. At the doorway, the Oracle of Life and Death stood while looking at their retreating backs until the rain and the distance concealed them. She stood there a moment longer, until someone called her name.

'Filomena!' It was Apolonio, who had been running errands in the town, a big black umbrella in hand.

'You!' Filomena pointed a finger at him as he briskly approached. 'You who say too few words! You keep information to yourself! You will be part of the downfall.'

'Stop talking,' said Apolonio, gently bringing down her outstretched arm.

'I saw you!'

'Saw me what? Where?'

'You were standing by when everything was about to be destroyed!'

'I don't know what you're talking about,' Apolonio said, trying to calm her down, worried that others might see them. He tried to make her go back inside the storage shed, so they could not be so visible.

'Don't push me.'

'I'm not pushing you. Let's go inside so the rain won't fall on us. Come on.'

Filomena shuffled backwards until they were in the centre of the storage shed. Apolonio closed the door behind them.

'You!' Filomena began to shout again.

'Don't shout. Do you want to wake people up?'

Filomena fell silent, looking at him suspiciously, her face half-turned away.

'Please come to my house tonight. I miss you.'

Filomena said nothing for several minutes, and Apolonio felt like his heart would break. Then she walked close to him and put her hands on the sides of his face.

'You said nothing, and because of that the hills walked to the house at Hacienda Marianita, and the house became hills.'

'Please come to my house tonight.'

She looked deep into his eyes, saw in them what could not be changed, and said, 'All right.'

On the street outside the storage shed, an owner-style jeep passed by, six men crammed inside. One of them was the unidentified man from Esperanza's debut soirée. The men, workers from Hacienda Marianita, were unsmiling and resolute. They were on their way to a meeting about an operation to be done on the grounds of the Arguelles house, an operation which some of them considered suicidal, but just might barely work.

Assumpta could not sleep during siesta on that rainy afternoon. All she wanted to do was to go to her secret room and spend the rest of the day there, writing, doodling, working on her maps theory, and thinking of its possibilities. What else can the disappearing maps make disappear, aside from places, houses and people? Can books written in the disappeared places also disappear once the places they were written in have disappeared? Can people, born in the places that eventually disappeared, disappear as well? She glanced over at Paz, who was deeply asleep, half her face under a pillow, and wondered how she could get past Mrs Palacio, who, sometimes, instead of sleeping during siesta, sat at a chair outside Guadalupe's room, reading.

But Assumpta really wanted to go to her secret room. While quiet in her bed after lunch with her family, she remembered something, a train of thought that she had a few days before, which trailed off eventually, and now she felt she could remember where to resume, but she had to see her drawings first.

She decided to take the risk. Mrs Palacio's arthritis got worse when it rained so she could have decided to stay in bed that afternoon. So Assumpta got out of bed, tiptoed past Paz's bed, and then across the bedroom of Guadalupe, who was also deeply asleep, prone on her pillow and lying very straight along the centre of her bed, her hands together across her breast, her sheets smelling of roses. Assumpta reached the door, and peeked out slowly. She could see no chair against the window in the corridor, and she silently squealed with joy. Now she could go to her secret room, but she would have to make sure that no one else saw her along the way.

She made her progress quickly and quietly. She took off her slippers and proceeded barefoot along the corridors of the bedrooms on the second floor, took the servants' staircase down to their quarters, ran past the cold tiles of the massive kitchen, past the pantry and the storage, and then finally came upon the short flight of stairs that led to her secret room. She took out the pencil stub that she used to keep the door closed, because the first time she found the room, the doorknob fell off in her hands, so in the meantime, the pencil stub idea worked to keep up the appearance that the door was still untouched, just in case someone else managed to find that hidden panel on the stairway.

She went to her small table, sat down on her little chair, and looked at a map of the house that she was drawing. All the rest of her maps and files and drafts had been relegated to the claw-foot bathtub at the centre of the room, arranged in piles.

The idea she was working on was that since she found out by exploring the house that there were more rooms in it than anyone actually knew, she also discovered that one particular corridor was also narrower than what it should be. When she knocked on the wood panels of that corridor, many of them sounded hollow. This was not at all like the corridors in the house at Hacienda Vida, where the corridors were wide, and when she knocked on the wooden panels, the person on the other side of it, usually a cousin, would actually hear her knock, emerge through the nearest door, and say hello.

At first, she thought it was the various closets on the inside of the second-floor bedrooms that muffled the sound of her knock on the corridor walls. After all, almost all rooms had wide and generous closets, there being an abundance of garments and undergarments and bed linens and drapes and pillows always in current circulation in the house, but she felt wrong about that idea. She also considered that there might already be part of the screened-in balcony beyond that hollow-sounding wall, but there wasn't. There was clearly something between the balcony and the narrow corridor. She thought maybe the hollow-sounding wall was actually one of the walls of that room at the end of the corridor, the one that has always been locked, but that bedroom was on opposite side of the hollow-sounding wall. When she knocked on the wall beside the door to the locked bedroom, it sounded muffled. That hollow-sounding corridor occupied her minds for weeks. She drew that portion of the house again, tried to measure it against her actual measurement of the corridor as it was, and still felt that something was amiss. The house actually had space that was unaccounted for.

Something was structurally different with this house. But then again the problem with Assumpta was that she was only seven-years-old, and being that small, there were things she could not logistically do, like pry open a wood panel in one of the corridors, or drill holes in the walls to make sure they were hollow. If she asked one of the menservants to do it, she would fall under suspicion and she would be forced to divulge her secret. But in the little, slow, faltering way of the growing though very observant seven-year-old that she was, she was able to deduce that there was about three feet of space between the two walls of the corridors that ran along the bedrooms and ended in Jacobo's bedroom, one wall hidden and the other faux, the one being seen by everyone and assumed as the real corridor wall. And she knew then that the answers to her questions lay within that one long stretch of secret corridor that was about three feet wide.

But then again, if it was indeed a secret corridor where all sorts of things were hidden, had the faux walls been built over the real walls after hidden objects were put in their places? Or was the faux wall built in order to give someone access to the secret corridor to sporadically place more objects in there and take some out? Three feet seemed like quite a narrow corridor, but a small-sized adult would just about fit through, if he slid along carefully and knew his way around. Assumpta further deduced that with that narrow and very long space, certainly it would not be furniture that would be kept in there, but very thin, stackable things, like paper, records, files, letters, and other important documentation that must be referred to every now and then while at the same time kept secret. And of course, too, somewhere within that corridor, there must be the map of the house, the very map that she had been looking for, the blueprint that would show where every single thing, room, door, closet, passageway, bathroom, storage area, and office lay.

Now that she had established, although just theoretically, that there was a secret corridor on the second floor of her house, she had to determine where the door to it was, so she could go in and see what was inside. There might be a key to that door somewhere, hidden in a similar manner as Sebastian's key, except that here even the door was hidden. She stood up from her little table and her little chair, and walked slowly around her secret room, her hands clasped behind her back, lost in thought, like a little adult, which she was actually turning out to be.

Assumpta, at seven-years going-on-eight in three weeks, was a born thinker. Even at a very young age, she had always tried to find out how things worked, and why they were there to begin with. Then she studied the schematics of certain machines, which required her to learn how to read much earlier than her siblings, and she managed to learn early how to read plain print, although cursive was still quite above her body of knowledge, a skill that, because of her lack of it, made her feel hindered. Also, she had the uncanny ability to find connections between and among a variety of things that seemed to have nothing to do with each other. So it was no surprise, really, that it was she who had figured out this mystery, and deduced that it existed to begin with.

But in her musings and her calculations, time went on, and soon, siesta time would be over. She opened the window pane a little, and saw that the rain had stopped, and some of the stable boys outside in her line of vision had begun to stir from their hammocks and cots, prepare coffee, and smoke. Quickly, she took off her slippers again, slipped out through the door, locked it close with the pencil stub, and then she was purely seven-years-old again as she ran and ran as fast and as quietly as she could, barefoot, back to her room, without being seen.

Back in her room, she saw that Guadalupe was still asleep and had not moved. To Assumpta, she looked like a wax statue of a saint, in the half-light caused by the closed curtains. Paz was also still asleep on her own bed, sprawled on her stomach. Assumpta saw that her own feet were dirty, which would give her away to Mrs Palacio, so she quickly went to the bathroom, washed her feet, towelled them dry, and went to bed and pretended to be asleep. But her heart was beating fast, not just from the run but from the realization that she was closer to what she had been looking for. So when three o'clock signalled the end of siesta, she was awake as ever, her mind and soul growing with fecund thoughts and premonitions.

Chapter 9

Interlude

In the Arguelles house, worries had to be set aside temporarily, as everyone was preparing for Assumpta's eighth birthday party, to be held in the outer gardens of the house. Everyone felt relieved, because it was starting to be quite tiring being cooped up indoors after weeks of almost-daily rains. August, however, was forecasted to be sunny. As for Assumpta, her reasons for relief were different. Since her discovery of the possibility of a secret corridor inside the house, for some reason she didn't want anyone else to walk that particular corridor, much less her friends from school who wanted to see her room every once in a while. Assumpta decided that for her party, no non-Arguelles should enter the house. She had begun to feel strangely protective of the house, and in her mind's eye, it had become a universe all its own and must be protected.

Margarita was only too glad to have a garden party such as this. As she grew older, her tolerance for the presence of children and the natural noise and disorder they brought had increased substantially. She was grateful that Assumpta, and Paz, for that matter, did not have the tendency to occupy too much of her time, and the way she considered things, the two small girls were the responsibility of Mrs Palacio, anyway, and silent, invisible, pre-pubescent Guadalupe was Mercedes's.

Yet, Margarita still had to deal with the preparations for this garden party for her eight-year-old daughter. Assumpta's birthday that year fell on a Thursday, which was a school day, so the party was scheduled on the Saturday afternoon following that. However, since it would not be of the same magnitude and importance of Esperanza's debut, and Assumpta didn't really care much about tiaras and necklines, Margarita actually decided to enjoy doing the preparations for Assumpta's party.

'Yellow-green,' Assumpta answered, when Margarita asked her what theme colour she wanted for the event.

Margarita was not expecting Assumpta to choose pink, but the actual choice was strange for her.

'Are you sure?' she asked Assumpta, forming her words slowly.

'Yes, Mama. I want a bright, wonderful, happy, yellow-green.' Assumpta said in a rather serious manner. 'Like the colour of little newborn leaves just sprouting from branches.'

'Why, hija?' asked Margarita, just out of curiosity, because she had no problems with the yellow-green and actually liked the idea herself.

'Because I am a leaf in the sun and wind and rain,' answered Assumpta, quite innocently, but with that strange wisdom that small children exhibit at the most unexpected of times, and then she kissed her mother on the cheek and ran off to the library, giggling.

Margarita tried to stifle a smile. She was a withdrawn, distant mother, but she always stepped up on the important occasions of her children's lives, as required of her by tradition. Assumpta was born five minutes after the end of the Feast of the Assumption of our Lady, but Margarita named her Assumpta anyway. And aloof and detached as she was, at times she could not help but be in awe of Assumpta's sense of humour and intuition.

Thus, still with the image of a tiny green leaf in her mind, she eagerly buckled down to work. The eighth birthday of any child was important, because that was the start of the age of obligation in the Roman Catholic Church. At eight-years-old, children had their First Holy Communion on December of that year, and were henceforth required to participate in all the obligations and requirements due to the church. So Margarita went to town and ordered a giant cake from the bakery, where she had a rather long and heartfelt discussion with the baker on what shades of yellow-green to use for the icing and the frosting, which the baker, because of the peculiarity of the request, agreed to do and actually started to be passionate about. Then Margarita went to the letterpress office and had a small batch of invitations and RSVP cards printed. Next, she commissioned the game facilitators and designed the tent layouts and the seating arrangements in the garden. The tents were to be white, with bright yellow-green stripes, and the tablecloths were to be an equally bright yellow-green, with large white polka-dots.

Margarita spoke to the head gardener and instructed him to be extra generous with watering the grounds, to not hesitate at all to get the soil muddy, just to make sure that on the day of the party, the garden would be green and healthy. Then she spoke with her head cook about the menu and talked to the servants that were to be assigned to the event. Most importantly, she talked to the guards, inviting both Tiyong Rotillo and Tiyong Pato to the meeting. Margarita certainly did not want a repeat performance of that spectacle during Esperanza's debut, which was no one's fault, really, but she didn't want to leave anything to chance, especially since the guests would be children, and they would thus be running around the grounds.

It was getting to be a particularly hot and sunny August, with the Agua de Mayo of three months ago suspended somewhere high, high up in the atmosphere, its former terrifying force rendered tired and depleted, and it would not descend for another year. Camarines was, in point of fact, preparing to deal with an incoming stifling, overwhelming, oppressive heat. El Niño, much more scorching than summer, was over Camarines like a thick, syrupy gas, blocking the cool breeze, letting only hot air through.

This kind of weather was a strange phenomenon in Camarines. The province, because of its geology, is more often battered by typhoons and heavy rains than with drought. Its land mass lay along the route of tropical depressions that form over the Pacific Ocean and travel towards Japan and China. Camarines has not had a drought for as long as the oldest person in the province, a retired school teacher by the name of Mrs Epifania Reyes, who was currently 102 years old and living with her great-grandchildren on the outskirts of the town, could remember. What she did remember were vicious typhoons with female names that brought flood and destruction two to three times a year, most of the time beginning in June. The soothsayers and false prophets, who set up their mini-stages in the town centre, prophesied hard times ahead and something indeterminate but of a ruinous nature. Because of the heat, they had to move their mini-stages from the centre of the square backwards, to take shelter under the awnings of the stores, from which the store owners consistently had to ask them to leave, and with which they often had to argue, and then pretend to place a curse on.

The putties keeping the glass panes in place in the windows of the stores, warehouses, mills, factories, and offices actually began to dry up and shrink, and with every harsh, hot whiff of air, the panels jiggled with a faint sound, like very small prisoners jiggling the bars of their cells, crying to be set free. Electric fans worked full time, and more of them were purchased by the wretched townsfolk. The local appliance store had to stock up on more electric fans, and raised their prices, supposedly to cover the special delivery they required of their suppliers, in order to get the fans into town at once, to meet the demand. Some electric bills soared as people actually stood in front of the open doors of their refrigerators, even with the electric fans already on, in an attempt to escape the sweltering heat.

Outside, not a cloud showed up for a few days. The sky stayed a consistent, harsh blue, the hue of lapis lazuli, forcing down angry heat on the mortals below, and the roads, sidewalks, and pavements radiated heat upwards. There was no escape from the heat. Every day, town maintenance personnel consistently picked up stray animals that had died from heat stroke. No one dared venture outside for fear of being burnt to a crisp.

Not even the powerful triumvirate of families that controlled the economic life of the entire Camarines was immune to the effects of the heat. Indeed, they had humongous houses designed for cross-ventilation, and an abundance of fans and refrigerators to help stave off the heat, but still the immaculate, fair skins of their Spanish pedigree became covered with a thin film of sweat. Jacobo himself had been sweating more profusely lately, and was always jittery. He had not been able to sleep well at night, and would often leave the house before dawn to visit his palay farms all morning, despite the heat, with his driver and encargados, and personal guards, only recently hired. Jacobo could not be at peace, and this heat was making his sense of unrest even more unbearable, as if something was pressing down on his chest, preventing him from taking deep breaths. He knew what it was, of course, it was not the heat, but he preferred to blame the heat.

As for the Visbales in the house at Hacienda Dolores in the town of Kamansi, they had all their drapes taken down, ordered all their window panes opened, and their bed linens changed

every single morning into soft white cotton sheets instead of
the heavy damasks that they were used to. Bolts of the fabric
came out of storage, were washed and dried, and placed on the
beds within the day. About a third of the electric fans in stock at
the local appliance store was purchased by the Visbales who, for
probably the very first time in their long lineage, realized that
they had pores in their skins from which sweat would come out.
Siesta was difficult to get through, the multitude of fans in use
per person notwithstanding, so they all went to bed earlier at
night, with all of the fans on full blast, until they began to feel
the heat on their skin again in the morning, at which point they
would get out of bed and start their day with cold drinks, and
the entire daily routine would unfold again.

So for the first time in perhaps a quarter of a century the
windows and doors of the house at Hacienda Dolores was
opened up to the world outside. Slow air, hot and muggy as
they were, finally travelled through the rooms and halls of the
house, clearing out the faint smell of mold and rot that had
accumulated over the many long years of darkness. The harsh,
slanting rays of the sun finally touched the surfaces of wooden
furniture that had been kept in the dark for so long that the
wood actually produced very faint cracking sounds at the touch
of the sun, as if rejoicing that they were finally being rid of the
moisture and mild putrefaction that had accumulated. For once,
the reflective surfaces inside the house—mirrors, chandeliers,
candelabras, doorknobs, picture frames, gildings—glimmered
and shone, and the whole house seemed to rise and expand and
glow with the heat wave. It seemed like an entirely different
house, lustrous, fresh, colourful, and lush with unexpected
and heretofore unknown youth and possibilities, and the heat
evaporated every single sliver of oldness from inside the house.
Completely exposed to the hot air of Camarines, the house

became nothing like the grand mausoleum it used to look and feel like.

The effect was not lost on the house's inhabitants. The dour, thin, slow-moving Visbales, Visbal-Visbales, and Visbales viudas de Visbal walked around their rooms in a mixture of awe and perturbation. Never before had they been so open and outside of their fortress-like habitat for more than a few hours, and they did not know how to handle it, but the house looked quite magical under the unusual light and the heat. They all felt quite incredulous that they had been living in that same house for years without seeing this magical shine and colour and life that have been hiding under the darkness—and their tall, long, thin, noses—all this time.

It was this curious new feeling of being reborn that made the Visbales decide to attend Assumpta's garden birthday party, and they promptly ordered the RSVP sent back to Margarita, signifying their attendance. The Visbales had the habit of steering clear of small children. The smaller the child, the farther away they should be. Even their own children, for generations, had been raised by equally long generations of nannies, people who had been employed by the family for a long time, with descendants who had never left the service and who, in fact, had inherited the posts of their siblings, parents, grandparents, and great-grandparents in the house at Hacienda Dolores.

Margarita herself was mildly stupefied at the arrival of the RSVP. She had sent them an invitation, with slots for ten persons, just out of tradition and respect, but she never expected them to willingly and consciously attend this particular party. Immediately, she went to her roll-top desk and looked for the list of names of the still-living Visbales, placing a check mark on the Visbal children she knew to be aged ten and below. There were only three. But counting their nannies and the adults who curiously agreed to come, it turned out that all ten slots would be availed of after all. Margarita put down her pen, put her hands up on her head to check if her hair was still in place, and looked out of her open, un-curtained window into the bright green garden outside, imagining the pale, thin, melancholic, snake-like Visbales frolicking in the sun with small children, including her Assumpta, and felt a faint, odd, unsettling feeling in her heart.

But whatever trepidation she had felt was all for nought, because the party ended up a success. Even the Visbales were uncharacteristically sociable, and talked so much more than they used to. They also laughed more often at the most subtle of prompts, and one of them even cracked a joke or two. The Monsantillos were as gay and forthcoming and genial as usual, but the Visbales being almost just as affable was something quite new, that both the older Arguelleses and Monsantillos found themselves looking at each other over the heads of the tall, thin Visbales, but only when these Visbales were seated, since they were all taller than everyone else. But Margarita herself did not want to dampen the event by investing an enigma on something that was probably nothing, so she shrugged off her confusion and went on managing the party, with food and the parlour games, and the Monsantillos wisely took her cue.

The Monsantillos already had their own worries on this day, because Beatriz had taken ill that same morning, and had not been diagnosed yet. Consuela had sent for a doctor, who would be coming to their house that evening, but for Assumpta's party, Consuela left Beatriz for a few hours in the care of Yaya Lina, who had been caring for all her children since they were infants and whom Consuela had called back from retirement specially for this purpose despite Yaya Lina's being sixty-eight years old. Consuela, like Margarita, was never the doting mother, having never been trained in how to care for small children. She entered her children's lives only after they had gone past their toddler years. Beatriz, just six, had been familiar with Consuela only for the past two years. At first, Consuela debated leaving Beatriz behind, but after all the rain, and after all the stress with Silvestre, she wanted to enjoy the sun and the half-hour drive from Mangkono to Toog, so she went with her family.

So on her birthday, in the year of the drought in Camarines, Assumpta got her sunshine and her leaves and her stripes and polka dots, and her parlour games and her huge three-tier cake covered with super-smooth yellow-green fondue icing. There were eight fat, leaf-shaped white candles set equidistantly around the last and widest tier of the cake, and one larger yellow-green candle. Jacobo lit the eight white candles. After everyone rose to sing 'Feliz cumpleano,' Assumpta blew all the eight candles, walking slowly around the cake as she did so. Everyone applauded and laughed with Assumpta as she applauded herself and jumped up and down and smiled with the innocence of one who knew only green fields and summer afternoons. And then Margarita went forward, lit the larger, yellow-green ninth candle, and then Assumpta walked forward to it, and closed her eyes to make a wish for the ninth year of her life that was beginning on this day. In her mind, she said, 'I wish the answers would reveal themselves to me. Por favor.'

After she blew out the ninth candle, the guests applauded again, and Margarita and Luningning began slicing the cake, and the servants walked around the table to serve the cake slices to the guests, together with the rest of the dessert. And as everyone laughed and talked and walked around, some in the shade, some in the sun, and commented on everything from the grass to the quality of the new chiffon fabrics to the latest news from Manila, to drapes and shoes and pencils and wine, and all sorts of disconnected things talked about during a gathering of people that know each other too much already, the sun burnt lower and lower in the sky, making people forget momentarily that there was to be a drought in Camarines.

Later that same day, after dinner, Assumpta and the rest of her family went to the sala, where all of her birthday gifts were brought after the party, and it was her time to open them all. Luningning had already sorted the gifts according to size, so that the smallest ones were to be opened first. Margarita was seated on one side of Assumpta on the large sofa to assist her in opening the gifts, while Mrs Palacio was seated on the other side of the sofa to list down the gift and the name of the giver, for use when the Thank You notes were to be sent out. Another servant was on the floor, tasked to arrange the opened gifts into boxes for temporary storage, until Assumpta and Margarita had decided what to do with them.

As expected, she got the usual range of toys, books, dresses, handkerchiefs, cologne, brush-and-mirror sets, several notebooks, several pen and pencil sets, several prayer books, and so many headbands, hair ribbons and hair clips. She opened a small packet wrapped in yellow-green but tied with a silk purple ribbon, and saw that it contained a small rosary with beads made of perfectly matched five mm white South Sea pearls and a crucifix in pinkish gold, which Margarita told Assumpta was called Russian gold. The centre medal featured the Lady of the Assumption, and it was also in Russian gold. The rosary, small enough for her hands, and just a little heavy, was presented in its own black leather box lined with yellow-green velvet. The velvet lining could be removed by tugging at a short ribbon tab. Hidden underneath the lining was a black silk pouch, embroidered with ANA, Assumpta's initials, in yellow-green. This gift was from Mercedes, of course, and Assumpta clapped her small hands and giggled her thanks in the direction of her grandmother. Mercedes smiled at the child from where she was seated, pleased that Assumpta liked her gift, which occupied

Mercedes' jeweller in Manila for a long time, matching all the pearls together in size, colour and lustre, before finally putting the rosary together. The box and the silk pouch had to be redone quickly, as Mercedes initially ordered them to be in pink, but when she found out that Assumpta wanted yellow-green, she immediately told her jeweller to craft new ones in the right colour. Assumpta closed the box gently and placed it beside her on the sofa.

From Margarita, Assumpta got a fountain pen small enough for her hands, together with a bottle of blue-black ink and a crystal inkwell in the shape of a leaf, and the entire set had its own box. These excited her. It meant she could now stop using the pencils that made her wrists ache after a while, and she did not have to use Jacobo's old fountain pens in the library, old ones that had become toothy for lack of use and were too big and heavy for her anyway. She could now draw her own maps with her own pen and ink. She hugged her mother, saying, '*Gracias, Mamita*,' and put the pen set aside, beside the rosary box.

Jacobo gave her A. A. Milne's *Winnie-the-Pooh* and *A House at Pooh Corner*, both first edition copies, which one of Jacobo's business managers spent about three months trying to find. Because by this time, and, in fact, right before she turned six, Assumpta already had full grasp of reading, and had since begun reading so fast and so much, surprising her entire family, Paz most of all, and not without the tiniest bit of jealousy. It was as if at a certain pre-ordained time in her life, a superpower within her was activated, and she devoured books upon books upon books, spending more and more time in her father's library, bringing more and more books into her secret room with the claw-foot bathtub. She often left the books in Jacobo's library in disarray, and so just to keep his own library neat and orderly—as well as to keep her off the philosophical treatises and monographs that he felt were too radical for a then six-year-old girl—Jacobo decided to start building her a library of her own, with age-appropriate books, all sanctioned and bought by him.

Assumpta had already been through Jacobo's more radical books before she turned eight, but as she was too young to even grasp the reality of a less-than-ideal world, even if the words showing these worlds were right in front of her, she continued with her comfortable, sheltered life unmarred by the painful texts she had read so far. But she had indeed read thick and dense books like a mountain goat could climb up rocky cliffs, and much faster. There were still so many words she could not understand yet, but at this point in her reading life, she could already find her away around works far more serious than those written for pre-schoolers. Sometimes, though, she wished she could read simpler things, because these grownup writers who were long dead took things too seriously. Even this Mr Charles Dickens, who wrote so nicely about ghosts, could use up three pages just describing the appearance of a chair that was being seen in the eyes of a character who was half-asleep. Thus, when she opened the wrapper and saw the two books, with their plain, brownish covers bearing the simple sketches of Christopher Robin and Edward Bear, she hugged them to her breast and jumped around and around for several seconds, laughing with gratitude at the honour of finally having a book to her own name. 'Gracias, *Papito*,' she called out to Jacobo, who was standing by the window near Mercedes. Jacobo smiled at her. Assumpta put the books beside the rosary box and the fountain pen set beside her on the sofa

The rest of the gifts were opened, and although Assumpta was polite enough, and effectively trained by Mercedes on the merits of keeping up basic social appearances, to express the requisite mild yet superficial appreciation at the gifts she beheld, they didn't evoke much emotion in her, so they were packed by the servant temporarily and put away somewhere where Margarita keeps unused gifts. But when Assumpta went to bed that night, the square leather box containing the pearl rosary, the long wooden case containing the fountain pen set, and the two new books were right beside her pillow, and she kept looking at them and caressing their surfaces, and she could not sleep for a long time, until it was already past midnight, at which point it was already a new day, and she was already living the very first hours of her ninth year. Before she drifted off to sleep, she thought of her maps, as usual.

One afternoon, deep during the same drought that had been hanging over Camarines for the past two months, Pacifico Visbal, eighty-one years old, the retired head of Hacienda Dolores, husband for fifty-five years to his second cousin Selina Suarez, father to four children, grandfather to nine, and great-grandfather to three, woke up after a fitful siesta and began chuckling for no reason at all. He began snickering even before he opened his eyes to the white heat of the mid-afternoon, and then he sat up in bed, still snickering. Still half asleep, he was not thinking of anything particularly funny, and was in fact trying to remember, while snickering, if he had had a funny dream, but none came to mind. His senses slowly woke up that way, his face contorted into a low laugh, and he reached out for the glass of cool water on his bedside table, and tried to take a sip, but he began to laugh harder and found that he could not stop.

He fell backwards and sat on his bed, trying to breathe deeply in between guffaws, and got the idea to hold his breath, hoping it would stop the involuntary laughter. It worked, but only for about two to three seconds, and the laughter came back with more ferocity. He felt his back starting to hurt and decided that he needed help. He stood up and tried to go to the door of his bedroom. The laughter caused him to double over, and he had to crawl to the door, and when he got there, his arms felt so weak that he couldn't lift it high enough to twist the doorknob. Instead, he banged on the door, laughing monstrously, and banged harder and harder, trying to stand but failing, trying to be heard by anyone in the house.

Chapter 10

Maladies

At that very same hour, in the house at Hacienda Vida, Salvador woke up from his siesta at exactly three o'clock, as had always been his habit. He was set to meet his administrators shortly in the sala, because together they would be inspecting the fish farm. Salvador had had a fitful siesta because of the intense heat, but by the time he got up, his mind was completely on the things that he had to do for the rest of the day. There was no point in putting them off, despite his constant weariness at the relentlessness of the tungro in his palay farm and the recent loss of a substantial stock of his abaca because of the negligence of his employees.

With these thoughts heavy on Salvador's mind, off they all went, at half past three, in two separate motor cars. Salvador was alone in his Berlina motor car with the old driver Busoy, who always drove very slowly, regardless of the road conditions and the purpose of the trip. It was no use asking him to go faster, as he would just say, 'Yes, Don Salvador,' and then lean resolutely forward in his seat, but his speed would never change. This used to irritate Salvador to some degree, but lately he had not minded at all. If his trips took longer than they should because of Busoy, that's still time spent away from other people, which Salvador found that he had been needing.

His house was not at peace. Beatriz was still ill, she had been sleeping longer and longer, and her affliction has remained undiagnosed even by the slew of doctors that Consuela had been calling to the house from Manila. Last time Consuela updated him on Beatriz's condition, she has been sleeping for up to twenty hours a day, and even Yaya Lina had moved her cot to Beatriz's room so she could care for the girl as much as possible. Beatriz would eat when she was awake and would sometimes ask for a particular dish. But she was awake at random hours, so the kitchen was required to be on its toes round the clock, the cooks working in shifts, ready to cook whatever food was requested through Yaya Lina and communicated to whoever was awake in the kitchen. Beatriz's undiagnosed illness was very distressing for Consuela, because the care of the children was supposed to be her dominion, and she felt she was failing in this regard. This distress in Consuela, which she could not communicate to her husband because she was fully aware that he was not to be bothered with maternal concerns, was nevertheless duplicated nightly in his presence, and the compounded amount promptly transferred to him, without the need for words.

Furthermore, Silvestre has been coming home from Ateneo de Naga more often than usual because of Esperanza, and was often seen in town with her on days when they should both be in school, which added more distress to the already-distressed Consuela. She constantly pleaded with Salvador to do something, as she felt that Silvestre, the person who was to take over the hacienda after Salvador, was Salvador's responsibility.

'*Por Dios y por santo*, Salvador!' Consuela would say in exasperation.

'He is a grown man,' Salvador would reply, 'but I will talk to him later.'

That had been their usual conversation almost every day for the past few weeks, but Salvador had never gotten around to doing what he said he would, partly because Silvestre was almost never home when he was, partly because he didn't know how to even begin talking to his own first-born son, but the biggest reason was that he considered Silvestre the least of his problems. If he doesn't save the hacienda, he might not even be able to fund the international travel that he had promised Silvestre after he graduated from the Ateneo, which was to be in a year's time, if he ever managed to graduate, considering his current preoccupations. The enormous task of saving the hacienda fell on his shoulders and his shoulders alone, and the isolation was not easy to bear. So he sat in the back seat of his motor-car, with Busoy driving at a snail-like forty kilometres per hour in the Berlina motor car on the open road to the fish farm, grateful for the time in the car that he could be quiet.

Hacienda Vida's forty hectare tilapia fish farm, most of it located in Barangay Labo in the town of Mangkono, was laid out in a wide and sprawling grid made up of pens, each measuring twenty square metres, with a metre's worth of ramps and mud paddies in between. The pens were about eight metres deep. Two-thirds of the pens were cemented, and a third had mud floorings. The cemented pens contained the larger, wider strain of tilapias preferred by restaurants in Manila. These were harvested only when they were fully grown, and then shipped in large iced trucks to the Manila warehouses of the suppliers that dealt with Salvador. The mud pens contained the tilapias of the smaller strain, were harvested younger, as preferred by the natives of Camarines and which are usually cooked into delicacies.

The management of the fish farm of Hacienda Vida was efficient and brisk, and harvest was done on a staggered basis, so that in any given week of the year, about three to five pens were being harvested. After the emptied pens were cleaned and checked for possible fungus growth, fresh fingerlings would be seeded into them the very next day, and the entire cycle would begin again.

For over a hundred years, this had been how the Monsantillos managed their fish farm, and it was Salvador who had added about seven more humble hectares to what used to be thirty-three hectares of fish corrals that existed before his time. So far, their system has always worked throughout the years, and the expansion was beneficial, and so Salvador did not feel the need to change anything in his current management system. The location of the fish farm was also a brilliant choice, being close enough to Lake Labo, to be able to use its fresh water without spending too much on irrigation installations and maintenance.

Bayani, the fish farm's encargado in Labo, and his head guard, the shotgun-bearing Noel, met Salvador and the rest of the party at the entrance. Bayani began to brief Salvador on the events of the past few days. On this particular day, no harvest was being made, but ten of the cemented corrals were due to be harvested within the week, and the harvest was to be immediately transported to Manila.

The ongoing El Niño had not affected the pens and the fish, as Salvador already knew, because the fish farm had an effective water system, but he felt a strange foreboding about his fish farm nonetheless. He could not help but feel afraid that something dark and decaying was afoot, as what had happened in his largest abaca warehouse, and he told Bayani to round up a group of men armed with scoop nets, because he wanted to go around and see the actual status of the fish and fingerlings himself. The fish farm in Labo was the one good thing in the hacienda remaining that did not need his saving, but still he felt that vague unrest in his heart, and somehow he knew that it had nothing to do with Silvestre.

Thus, with a map of all the fish pens in hand, including the feeding and cleaning and harvesting schedules, Salvador marched along the ramps, his small group of men following him behind in a single line like a ragtag squad of soldiers. The skies were completely clear, and the sunlight was a bright orange. It reminded Salvador of his afternoons alone in the Holy Rosary Minor Seminary, when he would wake up after the siesta hour. The sky outside usually looked exactly like that, and then he would be looking forward to Vespers, and then to dinner, and then to a night of long and heavy reading. Now, decades later, walking along the ramps of his fish farm with heavy burdens and strange, unidentified fears on his mind, he knew he had come a long way from that life, from that age, from that kind of freedom. He had long since realized that the seminario actually did not prepare anyone for the turmoils and vagaries of real life, because most of the time one had to make decisions contrary to one's theological erudition, so after he got his degree he never looked back, until now. Because now something evil was afoot.

But not in the fish farm. Their rather thorough inspection of all the corrals, which went on till well after midnight, revealed nothing anomalous, and for a moment Salvador finally allowed himself to breathe a sigh of relief, but it felt to him like a shallow relief. That he, after a very long time of burying his memories of his life and learnings in the seminario, suddenly recalled them all at this very moment was to him a sort of portent. He had no idea what it was going to be, so for want of something to hold on to, his heart fled back to what used to be a very comfortable, formulaic way of dealing with things.

Silently, he began reciting the oracion to San Benito, one of the multitude of prayers to the entire army of Roman Catholic saints that the seminario had taught him. That was seemingly a thousand years ago, and so the words faltered in his head as he tried to unearth the long-buried words from his heart and soul. But still he prayed on, over and over, pleading for insight on who was to poison him, when, and with what, so that he could avoid it as San Benito did. He hesitated over the Latin words and the Latin verbs as he walked with his men back to the main gates of the fish farm, in a single line once more, but with Salvador this time bringing up the rear, lost in stuttering prayer, feeling an icy cold grasp the corners of his heart, as he realized himself too weak to tell the Devil to begone.

At the very same moment, that same late night that Salvador Monsantillo was praying the oracion to San Benito, Esperanza was in her bedroom, sitting at her window seat, praying fervently, pleadingly to Santa Rita, something that she had never done before and that she also apologized for in the same prayers. Santa Rita, an Italian who had a terrible marriage but who nevertheless managed to turn her husband into a good person after many years of enduring his abuse, and who became an Augustinian nun after that same husband was murdered during a family vendetta, was assigned by the Roman Catholic church to be the patron saint of the impossible. When her two grown sons decided to avenge the murder of their father, Santa Rita prayed for divine intervention to prevent the act of vengeance, and it was granted, for her sons died of dysentery at seemingly just the right time. That Esperanza chose to pray to the patron saint of impossible causes instead of any other saint, even instead of the much more powerful Santa Maria, the Mediatrix, the Mother of God herself, was telling. She knew her request was impossible. She was pregnant and wanted not to be.

'Por favor, Santa Rita,' she said, uncharacteristically using Spanish instead of the English that she usually preferred and that she and Sofia Monsantillo had been taught in school, '*Lo siento, lo siento*. Santa Rita, *perdoname*, por favor.'

Her period had been delayed for three weeks, and it had never been late before this, but she had not told Silvestre yet, and not even Sofia, because, as impossible as her request was from the patron saint of impossible causes, part of her wanted to believe that the impossible would actually happen. Part of her wanted to believe that one day soon, preferably tomorrow, por favor, she would wake up and see the blood that would signify that the life she had been dreaming for herself, a life of travel and parties with a rich and famous husband, not Silvestre, could still happen. That, in her mind, was the possible, so her request could not truly be impossible, but a real possibility masquerading as an impossibility, and therefore must not be difficult for Santa Rita to grant, she who had turned her *sinverguenza* husband into a kind man but also prayed her sons dead. Esperanza might not like school, but she was good at twisting religious history to emotionally manipulate a saint when it suited her own ends.

But she was nevertheless sincere in her manipulation. She knew that if she just repented sincerely for her lack of chastity and showed more devotion to her prayers, and leveraged the past sufferings she had had to endure at the hands of others against her current request, the saints would look kindly on her and consider her deserving of the happiness and lifestyle that she wanted. This was how the Roman Catholic Church worked. Suffer at the hands of others, and a reward will come. Likewise, sin deliberately, but repent afterwards, and a reward will also come. She had sinned, indeed, but she is now repenting, and she also suffered a scandal during her debut soirée a mere four months ago, so surely she deserved this reward. If she just summoned the right kind of guilt in the right amount, and dealt with it with the right amount of spiritual torment, she just might get what she so fervently wanted.

'Santa Rita, por favor,' she said again, and continued her litany. Then she took a deep breath, brushed her hair one last time, turned off the lights, and went to bed. At the end of the hall, in Jacobo's dark, quiet bedroom, a window opened.

Mercedes, inside her bedroom, sleepless in her old age, was praying the santisimo rosario on her rosary beads made of sterling silver, and with a centre medal engraved with the image of La Virgen de Guadalupe. It was a gift to her from her parents when she had her First Holy Communion at the age of eight. Back then, it was called Primera Comunion, and all of the rituals were conducted in Spanish, within a two-hour-long mass. But after the Americans came, English gradually crept into almost everything, including the Santa Misa, that language so uncouth and disagreeable, with its nouns completely sexless, and with terribly chaotic tenses. Mercedes never warmed to English, and although she had a grasp of it from reading the dual-language newspapers that sprouted in the country after the war and made their way to Camarines, she made it a point never to speak it, even when talking to bank employees and accountants. Instead, she would address them in a mixture of Spanish and Bicol, which she liked, because so many Bicol words were actually Spanish. Sometimes Tagalog words would emerge from the thick, robust intonations of her speech, a remnant of her Caviteña roots, but she was always quick to check herself, and as time went by, her slips became more and more rare. Over time, she had turned herself into a Spanish-speaking Bicolana.

'Santa Maria, Madre de Dios, *ruega por nosotros pecadores*,' she muttered, the words long embedded into her system. '*Ahora y en la hora de nuestra muerte*. Amen.'

The words to the formulaic prayer had been memorized by generations of Roman Catholics in the Philippines, and had not changed for centuries. While other translations had been made in different parts of the country, such as the Bicol '*Tara, Cagurangnan* Maria,' Mercedes faithfully stayed with the Spanish version. Having prayed it several times a day for so long since she was eight, the daily frequency having increased as she grew older and had less and less of other things to do and fewer and fewer hours of sleep to take, she knew that if she ever turned into a rock, and someone broke her body open, inside they would find carved the words to 'Ave Maria'.

The santisimo rosario is a single prayer composed of a long string of repeated memorized short prayers, and the purpose of the rosary beads was to keep track of the sequence and number of the short prayers. There are five decades in the santisimo rosario, and each decade is composed of one 'Padre Nuestro', ten 'Ave Marias', and one 'Gloria'. Each decade is dedicated to each of the five mysteries assigned to a particular day of the week by the Roman Catholic Church. On Sundays, Wednesdays, Saturdays, and religious holidays, the Glorious Mysteries are the focus. On Mondays and Thursdays, the Joyful Mysteries are invoked, and on Tuesdays and Fridays, the Sorrowful Mysteries take their turn. It was a Tuesday, so Mercedes muttered from memory, which also operated completely in Spanish, the Misterios Dolorosos, the set of mysteries that was supposed to follow the agony and death of Jesucristo. With each prayer there must be a deep meditation on the magnitude of the sacrifice that had been made to save mankind from sin, in a long prayer composed of a total of fifty-one short prayers, but after centuries of memorization, it had become a mere compliance for the people of Camarines, a show of obedience, made to display a piousness to others. In the case of Mercedes, it was a display of piousness to herself, and that display gave her comfort.

She ended her prayer, kissed the crucifix, kissed the centre medal that held an engraving of La Virgen de Guadalupe, and dropped the rosary into her pocket, the only material possession remaining of her youth in Cavite, an artefact that has been living inside her pocket for more than eight decades, made of silver, which was said to be used to make weapons against creatures of the underworld.

Suddenly she heard a gunshot ring through the quiet house. And then she heard another. She closed her eyes, fearful, and muttered the 'Ave Maria' once more, for the fifty-fourth time within that same hour.

In his bedroom, Jacobo stood with a revolver in his right hand, looking down at the man he had just shot. The man was on the floor, not moving, blood gushing from two gunshot wounds on his chest. A moment later Margarita ran in, saw the dead man, and screamed. Mercedes heard the scream from her bedroom and uttered a fifty-fifth 'Ave Maria'. The dead man on the floor was the unidentified man who had barged into the ballroom on the stormy night of Esperanza's debut soirée.

It was not an easy night to get through for the rest of the people in the house at Hacienda Marianita. Mrs Palacio was made to sleep in Assumpta's bed, while Assumpta slept beside Paz, in the bedroom inside Guadalupe's. Inez and Jacobo II were made to sleep in makeshift cots inside Margarita's room, and manservants were made to stand guard outside each occupied bedroom. Jacobo did not stay in his bedroom. He spent the rest of the night in his office, away from the rooms where his family was sleeping, accompanied by three of the guards from the grounds. The rest of the servants, especially the maids, were terrified of being left alone, so they huddled together in one bedroom.

The very next morning Jacobo hired personal guards, aided in his selection by the Chief of Police of the town of Toog, who also immediately, resumed the investigation regarding the identity of the man, an investigation that began after the soirée but never really moved forward for lack of leads. But the man was still unidentified, even after having been held in the town morgue for a week, while summons for relatives and friends to come forward and identify him were plastered on the walls and street lights of the town. The summons bore a picture of the face of the dead man, and people did not even bother to look. Only Filomena seemed to know anything about the man, because when she saw one of the summons posted on the outside wall of the rice mill where her second husband worked, she pointed at the picture and shouted, 'It cannot be stopped!'

Mercedes had been keeping Marianita's letters under the shawls that were stored inside the chest of drawers in her bedroom. She had not read them since she had taken them out of the safe deposit box at the bank, as she knew what they said. She has read them before, after they were given to her by her mother-in-law, Barbara dela Costa, wife of Antonio Arguelles, who, in turn, had received them from her mother-in-law Esmeralda, wife of Enrique Arguelles. Esmeralda was the one who found the letters among Marianita's things after Marianita died, when she was going through the dead woman's clothes looking for a suitable dress for her to wear while being displayed inside the casket. Esmeralda read the letters once and never read them again, and decided never to mail them, even though the name and address of the person they were for were clearly written on the envelopes. The very moment she made that decision she had become the custodian of the letters, and became the very first in the line of custodians, the current of which was Mercedes who, as Jacobo II was yet unmarried, had no one to pass the letters to. Even if she wanted to mail them, the letters would be returned to her, as she heard that the person the letters were meant for had died long ago, a few years after Marianita died. Hence, there was no way for Esmeralda's successor to reverse Esmeralda's decision. Esmeralda was able to pass on only her custodianship of the letters, but never her decision not to mail them. This was why her spirit was regretful and could not rest in peace.

As far as Mercedes knew, the contents of the letters were known only to Esmeralda, Barbara, and herself, Arguelles women who had no Arguelles blood in them. It was an unspoken rule, understood by all these women, that they would safeguard the letters from Arguelles eyes, which was the original intention of Marianita. Now Mercedes felt it was time to pass on the letters to Margarita. She had delayed passing them on for some reason, but she was weary and old. She went to her armoire and took out the letters, the individual envelopes carrying each letter housed in a bigger envelope, which was Barbara's doing. She walked to Margarita's bedroom and knocked on the door. Margarita told her to enter, and she did. Margarita was sitting at her small desk near the corner of the room, going through some documents.

'Hija,' Mercedes said to Margarita, walking to her, holding the envelope in her outstretched hands. 'I have been guarding this for years. I have been keeping it in a safe deposit box. But now it's your turn.'

'What is this, Mama?' Margarita said, taking the envelope and turning it over, opening the flap, and peering inside. 'Please, have a seat,' she gestured at the chair near her.

'Those are letters written by Doña Marianita,' Mercedes said, sitting down. She was starting to feel a slight lifting of what had always been heavy on her shoulders for decades.

'Letters? To whom?' Margarita looked at her mother-in-law, confused.

'The man is long dead,' Mercedes said, trying to sound final. 'We can no longer mail them. But we need to keep the letters,' Mercedes took a deep breath, and once more said, more pleadingly, 'We need to keep the letters.'

'I don't understand, Mama,' Margarita, said, closing the flap on the envelope and handing it back to Mercedes.

'Read them, hija.' Marcedes gently pushed Margarita's hand, with the envelope, back. 'Please read them. Then you will know what to do.'

'*Esta bien*, Mama,' Margarita said, still puzzled, but now curious. 'I will read these.'

'Mama Barbara gave them to me, and Doña Esmeralda gave them to her. Now they are yours,' said Mercedes, her shoulders feeling even lighter now. 'I trust that you will guard them well, and then pass them to the next one at the right time.'

'I will, Mama. *Gracias para la confianza*,' Margarita said, holding the envelope to her breast.

Then Mercedes stood up and walked away from the letters and her duty to Marianita, and felt even lighter, but it was not relief. Instead, it was a deep, tremendous sadness.

Margarita, however, was not as careful a custodian as Mercedes and the others who came before. She did not read the letters right away, and so did not think of hiding them right away. She had kept them on top of her small desk for days before remembering to read them, as she was very bothered by Esperanza's unacceptable activities, such as skipping school to be with Silvestre without a chaperone, and Jacobo's increasingly distant manner, which she originally wanted but now did not like, in light of the current scandal. She needed a partner to deal with this crisis, and Jacobo was not being one for her. She did eventually read the letters, and then understood why she had to hide them, to be passed on to the next non-Arguelles blooded Arguelles wife, presumably Jacobo II's future wife. But on one of those days that Barbara's envelope carrying Marianita's letters was still sitting on top of Margarita's dresser, looking as quotidian as her bottles of perfume and jars of cream, Guadalupe, a full-blooded Arguelles, the very kind of person that was not meant to read the letters, walked in and read them.

All the other children in the house seemed oblivious to everything else that was unfolding around them. Jacobo II remained dutiful in his role as the first-born son, which was to stay in school at the seminario and accompany Jacobo on errands when he was on a school break. He was obedient to and unquestioning of this fate. Inez, who knew the hacienda had no demands on her like they did on Jacobo II, roamed the fields as often as she could when there was no school, sometimes on her bicycle and sometimes on horseback. And Paz, the one with no magic in her soul, managed to turn ten years old in the house at Hacienda Marianita without keeping any secrets.

Lately, Assumpta had been noticing that her eye was turning blurry. At first she thought it was only strain, because she had been reading so much. It took her months, but she finally found out some of what Sebastian's papers said. It looked like an entry in someone's diary, as they sounded like they were telling the story to themselves. Someone named Lorenzo Monsantillo killed a Joselito Visbal because Joselito wanted to steal from Lorenzo a woman named Pilita Arguelles. This Pilita refused to marry Lorenzo, and she took poison, which did not kill her right away but made her very thin and ugly until she died, and then Lorenzo Monsantillo gave half of his money to the father of Pilita. Assumpta was not sure she was translating the words correctly, though. At that moment none of it made sense to her, and she wondered why no one told the police that Lorenzo killed Joselito and caused Pilita to kill herself. To Assumpta, all of eight-years-old, these were very strange stories that happened only in fiction but not in real life. Then she thought maybe someone was indeed writing a fictional short story and was just using last names that were familiar to her, although that didn't explain why Sebastian held on to these papers.

She was actually more bothered by the strangeness of her eyesight. She could tell that the blurring was only in one eye, because when she covered her right eye, she could read everything clearly with her left eye, from the book she was reading to the posters that were on the walls of the classroom. But when she covered her left eye, everything was a massive blur with her right eye, as if she was seeing things through frosted glass. There were only coloured blobs, with no distinct lines to distinguish one object from another. That's when she thought she was going blind.

'Mama, I am going blind,' she blurted out suddenly one evening during dinner.

'Ay, Santa Maria!' Margarita said, understandably startled. 'How can you tell?'

'I can't see from my right eye, Mama,' Assumpta said, covering her left eye with her hand. 'It's all a blur. I can't even see you this way.'

'What happens if you cover your right eye?' Jacobo II asked, peering across the table at Assumpta's small face. 'Can you see me?'

Assumpta transferred her hand to cover her right eye. 'I can see you clearly with this eye.'

'What happens when you don't cover any of your eyes?' Inez asked. She put her face inches away from Assumpta's.

'Of course I can see you clearly when you're that close,' Assumpta laughed.

Inez walked to the wall and stood with her back against it. 'Here, how do I look when you don't cover any of your eyes?'

'It's like there's two of you, one in front of the other. One is clear and the other still looks like you but is blurred.'

'Look at me, too!' Paz said, jumping up from her chair and standing beside Inez.

'You have a ghost standing in front of you that looks exactly like you,' Assumpta said, laughing, and Paz pretended to be scared while Inez laughed.

'Come back to the table, Inez, Paz, por favor, and finish your dinner,' Margarita said. And to Assumpta, she said, 'Tomorrow I will take you to the doctor.'

Guadalupe was silent the whole time. Jacobo, on the other hand, was not there that evening. He was at the house at Hacienda Dolores in Kamansi because Pacifico Visbal, who started laughing three weeks ago and could not stop, had finally died, and he died laughing. His son, Matias, had called both Jacobo and Salvador on the telephone, asking them to come right away, and they did. Jacobo was able to arrive first, and Salvador did depart for Hacienda Dolores right away, but he always took time before arriving, on account of Busoy's driving. While in transit, no one could reach him, so Bayani could not tell him that all of the fish in the fish pens in Labo had died.

Chapter 11

The Fire

It was the most stifling December Esperanza had ever experienced, and she wanted to fret about her looming wedding day, but she couldn't, because her morning sickness, which she was told was supposed to happen only within the first trimester, was still ongoing in her fourth month. She looked at herself in the mirror of her dresser, alone in her bedroom at the house at Hacienda Marianita, and decided that she looked hideous. Her skin was red and flushed, and not in a healthy way, as if she were sun-kissed like the glamorous women she saw in her magazines vacationing in Monaco where Grace Kelly was just installed as a princess. On the other hand, she, Esperanza, looked like she was having an allergic reaction to something, and she thought that maybe this entire situation was what she was allergic to, this heat, her weight gain which was all in the hips and thighs, the wedding that was to happen in less than a week, and Silvestre, that man to whom she would be chained forever, and this hot, humid, unbearable land that he had to stay in, with her by his side as his wife until the hour of their death. All of these were conspiring so that she would not be able to explore her full potential as a woman of the world. She thought of Grace Kelley, and her anger at Silvestre spiked.

She fumed, picked up her brush, and started brushing her hair, which used to be soft and curly but had become stiff and tightly coiled, tangled, and knotted. She had been keeping her hair up in a bun during the day because of that and because of the heat, but in the evenings, after dinner, she would still turn her hair loose and hope that by some miracle it would be back to its normal, beautiful state. Nothing like that happened, and on this particular night, less than a week before her wedding to Silvestre, Esperanza decided that she had to stop hoping for miracles, as they never happened for her. Santa Rita de Cascia had failed her by making her remain pregnant against her will, and now her own skin and hair had turned themselves against her.

'Madre de Dios,' Esperanza muttered under her belaboured breath. This time it wasn't a pleading to a saint but an imprecation to a power higher than that of a saint. No more por favor, gracias, and esta bien.

Margarita walked in. 'How are you?'

'I hate my hair!' Esperanza threw her hairbrush on top of her dresser, hitting some bottles and toppling them over.

'Now, now, stop fretting,' said Margarita, as she tidied Esperanza's things. 'I remember when I was pregnant with you, it wasn't pretty either.'

Esperanza was quiet, and just looked straight at her red face and unruly hair in the mirror.

'I had pimples all over my face and neck,' Margarita said, 'and I couldn't cover it up. The only makeup I could buy here was those face powders that felt like flour and smelt like decaying tea roses.'

Esperanza remained quiet as she let her mother ease the tangles in her hair. She could see Margarita's resolute face in the mirror, looking intently at her hair as she worked the hairbrush through the ends of her hair a few times, gently, and then moved up a few inches.

'Pregnancy is never pretty, but the good thing about it is that it's just temporary,' Margarita said.

'It's marriage that's permanent,' said Esperanza, looking down at her fingernails.

Margarita stopped what she was doing, but only for a moment, although her daughter still noticed that.

'You will do well with Silvestre. The Monsantillos are a good family. You will be taken cared of very well.'

'That's not what I'm after, Mama,' Esperanza sighed, still looking at her fingernails, and then gave out a deep, loud sigh, which, for once, was not theatrical or overdramatic.

'You need to adjust your dreams to your situation, hija,' Margarita said gently as she resumed brushing Esperanza's hair.

'Shouldn't it be other way around?' Esperanza asked plaintively, now looking at her mother through the mirror. 'Adjust our situation to our dreams?'

'No,' Margarita replied firmly. 'You cannot make your dreams come true unless your entire environment allows it.'

There was a heavy silence between the two of them for several minutes, punctuated only by the sound of hair being brushed, and the sounds of the night—birds, crickets, frogs—wafting in through the window that was open to the stifling summer.

Finally, Esperanza broke the silence. 'Mama,' she said, then hesitated.

'What is it?' Margarita prodded after a minute.

'Are you happy with Papa?'

Margarita paused, taken aback by such a simple question. 'I have been happy, but now I am too old to require happiness,' Margarita said, trying to remember happy times with Jacobo and remembering only very little. She must not have been happy for a very long time. 'What I need at my age are safety and care, and your Papa provides those for me.'

'I'm not old as you yet, Mama,' Esperanza said, looking at her own face in the mirror.

'I know, querida, but you will get there,' Margarita said, trying to keep her face expressionless even as she felt a tug at her heart at the thought of her beautiful daughter becoming old and unhappy, although safe.

'I'm not sure that I want to,' Esperanza whispered, but her mother heard her. 'You must. That is the direction your entire world now wants you to take.'

'What does the world know? What if I don't want to go there?' Esperanza whispered again, knowing that her mother would hear her, as she always did.

'It will be painful,' Margarita said, then put the hairbrush down on the dresser. 'Choose sadness over pain. Pain makes you ugly, but there can be beauty in sadness.' Then she kissed Esperanza on the cheek and left. It was only after her mother had left the bedroom that Esperanza realized that neither of them ever mentioned love. That moment, deep in the drought of Camarines, Esperanza was changed forever, but she did not feel the house when it heaved, ever so slightly, for her.

Assumpta, on the other hand, felt that same heaving, in her secret concrete room with the claw-foot bathtub. She looked up from what she was doing, and looked around, wondering if she got dizzy. She held her head in her hands, shook her head gently from side to side, but did not feel dizzy, so it certainly must not have been her new strange vision with her one remaining good eye. But there was a heaving, of that she was certain. She stood up to look out the window towards the stables and saw that nothing seemed to be amiss. She stood still for several more seconds, her legs far apart, wondering if she would topple over, but she didn't, so she walked back to her papers and her maps that were spread out all over the floor, and resumed her wondering about why the maps of the house that she drew only months ago were already faded.

She sifted through them and rearranged them on the floor according to the date that she drew them, which she had scribbled at the bottom of each sheet. One set of maps in particular was more faded than the others, and this was the set she had drawn of the second floor of the house, when she was trying to figure out why one of the corridors was narrower than what she thought it was supposed to be. This was the corridor that ended in a room that had always been locked and no one knew what was inside it, not even Mercedes when Assumpta asked her, and not even Jacobo when Assumpta asked him. What was strange about the fading of her maps was that only the lines representing the corridor were faded. The rest of the lines were still dark and clear.

She looked through her maps of the first floor, and saw that the part where the sealed-off back sala was had faded. In another sheaf, she saw that her drawings of the third floor, which contained only Sebastian's office but was now being used by Jacobo, had completely disappeared, and so had her drawings of Sebastian's bedroom on the fourth floor. She stacked the papers together. At the bottom was the back sala, on top of it was the area of the narrow corridor with part of the screened-in balcony next to it, and then on top of it was the office, and at the topmost was Sebastian's bedroom.

Assumpta sighed, propped her forehead on her fingers the way she saw Jacobo do it a million times when he was tired, and felt her one remaining good eye starting to ache. Her eyestrain, more common now, was preventing her from doing her work, but she knew she had to stop. She gathered her papers, placed them inside the briefcase, left her secret room and went to her own bedroom that she shared with Paz so she could wash up and go to sleep.

Later that night, in her room, Mercedes could not sleep, as usual. She had been feeling the house heaving all evening, and she felt a dreadful, sinking feeling in her heart that what was destined to happen would soon come to a full finish, and even though she had known this for decades, she decided she still was not ready. She knew she would never be ready, despite her efforts to be accepting of her lot, and her advanced age only made her grow weaker instead of stronger. If fate still required her to be witness to all that would unfold, she knew she would either go insane or die a very undignified death, and such a death, to her, was not what she deserved.

She walked to her armchair, which, recently, she had one of the maids adjust to face the window. Lately, Mercedes had wanted to envision her eventual freedom from the house at Hacienda Marianita each time she prayed the rosary, and looking out at the window to the hot and stifling hills of the hacienda somehow helped.

'I have been obedient,' she said to the slow, hot breeze that was wafting in through her window. 'I have been careful. I have done all that I have been told to do.'

She took out her rosary beads from her pocket and made the sign of the cross. 'I deserve to be spared,' she said, and began praying for exactly that. While uttering the monotonous invocations in her decades-old Spanish, she thought of her husband Alfonso, and of Jacobo, and of Jacobo II, and then of Esperanza, who she had foreseen growing to be the opposite of what she used to be, disdainful of love before she even begun to know it, disdainful of life before she had even truly begun to live.

It was a Thursday, so Mercedes prayed the Joyful Mysteries as set by the Roman Catholic Church. The First Joyful Mystery was the Annunciation of the Angel Gabriel to Mary. Mercedes closed her eyes, tried to envision the scene that she had seen depicted many times and in many styles in various books, pamphlets, and estampitas, but all she could see was Esperanza, standing in front of Gabriel, wearing a shapeless pink gown, her long, curly hair waving about her head, her face contorted in a pain that was beyond the physical, and Mercedes knew Esperanza would never recover from what she had gotten herself into, despite Jacobo's power. Every single one of them, including Jacobo, moved only within the precious, throbbing, flaming bubble of what this house allowed, despite their illusions that they can choose their own fate.

Mercedes continued her rosary dutifully, and throughout all of the other four Joyful Mysteries, she tried her best to envision Santa Maria and the Santo Niño Jesucristo, and the joy that was required in her heart upon the invoking of the Joyful Mysteries, but her mind always went to Esperanza, in excruciating, repulsive, irrevocable pain. But she nevertheless finished praying the rosary, as she always does regardless of the situation, made the sign of the cross, kissed the crucifix of her rosary beads, and dropped them into her pocket. She stood up from her chair and walked two steps closer to the open window, waiting for a voice.

'I deserve to be spared,' she repeated to the slow, hot breeze while looking out into the darkness. She knew what was out there, as she had seen it a million times from this bedroom where she had been staying since Alfonso died, and Jacobo and Margarita moved to the much bigger master bedroom, the same one from which Margarita kicked her husband out eventually. She liked this bedroom. It was smaller, but the windows were bigger. The bed here was also not as massive, so she did not need that step stool each time she had to get in and out of bed. Over the years living in that bedroom with Alfonso she never got used to using the step stool, and had asked him to have the bed legs shortened for her, but he just waved the request away as too inconsequential for him. Mercedes, sworn to obedience and who had imbibed the warning of 'Cuidado', dropped the matter, but many years later, when she realized she could move to a different bedroom, she was relieved. That master bedroom had seen the death of several Arguelleses, and Mercedes did not want to die there.

'I heeded your warning,' Mercedes whispered. The air still felt hot on her skin, but she began to feel a slight cooling. After a few minutes, something cold and light touched her face.

'Bueno,' a voice whispered into her left ear. It was very soft, but quite audible.

'Gracias,' Mercedes whispered back. She walked out of her bedroom door to the corridor, the hinges of her door barely making a sound in the stillness of the night. She looked at the floor and saw a faint glimmering there, starting from where her feet were and then moving forward in stripes, slowly, like a guide. Mercedes took a step forward.

'Bueno,' she heard the voice in her left ear again, and took another step forward, and then another step, and then another, all the while looking down to see where the glimmer was leading her, her slippered feet noiseless on the old, polished wood.

Eventually, she reached the corner where the corridor split to the right, where the master bedroom was, and to the left, where at the very end there was a room that had been locked even before Mercedes came to Hacienda Marianita. The glimmer was leading her there, and she followed. The corridor was long and much narrower here, as noticed by Assumpta months ago, and it was hardly ever used, but the glimmer was slow, and so was Mercedes, to whom it felt like a wedding march, because the cadence was the same. As she continued to walk, head down, watching the glimmer move forward in stripes, her mind went to Paz, and in her mind Paz was standing by a window, with large black hollows for eyes, and then flames grew from the floor and engulfed her and the wall behind her.

Mercedes shuddered at the vision but continued resolutely with her slow, macabre march, guided by the glimmer, for several more steps, but even before she got to the end of the corridor the glimmer stopped moving forward on the floor, and went to the wall to her left, the pattern rising slowly in vertical striations. Mercedes faced the wall, and her hand went to her pocket to lightly touch the rosary there. She waited a few minutes, and then walked into the glimmer in the wall. The house heaved and sighed, and by the time the glimmer disappeared completely, so had Mercedes.

The next day, Guadalupe, who had not seen her grandmother all morning, knocked on her door, and when no answer came, she opened the door and walked in, and instantly knew that Mercedes was gone and would not be coming back.

Guadalupe, over the past few months following her discovery of Marianita's letters, had grown increasingly quiet and invisible. She told no one of what she had read, as was her habit, but the knowledge of what Marianita had gone through, in secret, was now also her burden, and also a secret. She had become even more inward than she used to be. Her newfound knowledge made her more analytical of every single detail she noticed in the house, every dark corner, ever word whispered that she could overhear by accident through walls and floors. Even from her bedroom, she could hear Mercedes muttering her rosary through her bedroom door, and Jacobo talking to people in the library. She could hear Assumpta shuffling her papers somewhere in the house, Esperanza talking to Margarita, Margarita talking to Luningning, the maids chattering and giggling.

At first, Guadalupe was overwhelmed by the sound, which happened all over and all at once, but she quickly learnt how to quell the cacophony by focusing on only one particular sound— something that served to noticeably muffle all the others, until she decided to focus on another sound, which then muffled the previous sound together with the rest. That was how she found out about Jacobo's failing negotiations with his employees, and how much he has been paying the Chief of Police as stipend for protecting his interests.

One night, she was in bed while listening to Margarita in the living room downstairs. She was talking over the telephone with whom she assumed to be an extremely unhappy Esperanza, one week married and still complaining about her pregnancy, her growing distance from Sofia, and her terrible relationship with the rest of her in-laws. Suddenly, a specific sound, although slighted muffled, caught her attention.

'Go. Go and do it,' a man was saying in a low voice.

'I am afraid,' a woman replied. Her voice hushed and tentative.

'This is your job. You promised you would do it.'

'I know, but they have been good to me.'

'If you don't do it, someone else will, and you will have to answer for your refusal to do what you have been told to do,' the man's voice sounded more gruff now.

There were several minutes of silence. Guadalupe squinted, trying to make out the next voice.

'All right' the female voice said, her voice laced with uncertainty.

'Tonight. You already have the matches and the kerosene.'

'Yes.'

Guadalupe bolted upright in her bed, panting heavily, her heart pounding such that she could hear the sound magnified in her ears, as if her heart were in all of the rooms in the house and she could hear all of them pounding together in unison.

She tried to quell the sound of her multiplied heartbeats while she tried to listen for the conversation she had just overheard. She wanted to figure out who the woman was so she could be stopped.

'Did you hide them well?' the man asked.

'Yes,' the woman replied. 'I have been hiding them behind the laundry bins.'

Guadalupe then knew who the woman was. 'Elena,' she blurted, and jumped out of bed, to wake Jacobo. She ran, barefoot, out of her room, shouting, 'Papa! Papa!'

When she got to Jacobo's bedroom, she barged in and found Jacobo just getting out of bed. '*Que barbaridad!*' he shouted. 'Guadalupe, what is going on?'

'Papa!' Guadalupe panted, 'Elena is going to burn the house!'

'Por dios y por santo, where did you get that?'

'I heard it! I heard her!'

Jacobo was flabbergasted, and didn't really understand completely what was going on, but after the recent attempt to murder him, he did not want to leave this instance to chance.

'Who is it again?'

'Elena!'

'Elena?' Jacobo did not know who Elena was.

'*La lavandera*, Papa!'

'Ay, dios mio! Get your mother now! Wake everyone up and stay together!' Jacobo took his revolver from under his pillow and went to get Jacobo II, while Guadalupe ran to Margarita's bedroom.

Jacobo and Jacobo II ran down the staircase and then to the back of the house where the laundry area was, shouting Elena's name, but there was no one there. Jacobo sniffed the air, and smelt kerosene and smoke, but there was no smoke in the room.

'Do you smell that?' Jacobo asked Jacobo II.

Jacobo sniffed the air. 'Yes.'

They went around the room quickly looking for the source of the smell, but Jacobo immediately said, 'It's not here.'

Then they heard glass shattering. They ran out of the laundry area and saw that the wall that sealed the back sala was already going up in flames. A woman was there, throwing flaming rags at different portions of the wide wall.

'Stop! Elena!' Jacobo shouted, but for a moment his heart was gripped by the cold memory of the multong vengativa that he saw in his room on the night of Esperanza's debut. Some of the servants had heard the noise and had come out of their quarters. Some of the female servants screamed and then ran back out. By this time Jacobo's guards, stationed right outside the house, had come in upon hearing the glass shattering and the screams.

'Don Jacobo!' they shouted. 'We will get water!' And then they ran back out, every single one of them forgetting their duty to protect the physical body of their employer.

'Elena, stop or I will shoot you!' Jacobo shouted, pointing his revolver at Elena and cocking the hammer.

'Papa, no!' Jacobo II held his father's arm.

'Move away,' Jacobo said to his son and pushed him away. 'Stay back.' The fire was taller and wider now, and was starting to roar. Jacobo placed his forefinger on the trigger.

'Elena, if you don't stop, I will shoot you!' Jacobo shouted.

'Papa, no! No shooting! We must stop the fire!' Jacobo II clutched his father's arm again.

Elena did stop, but her dress, which may have had kerosene spilt on it by accident, caught fire, and she began to scream. Jacobo, his revolver still pointed at Elena, could not move. Both he and Jacobo II were transfixed, Jacobo thinking about the multong vengativa, while Elena spun around, trying to tamp down the flames on her dress, but ended up spinning straight into the fire that she had made. Her screams did not stop for several minutes as the fire grow taller, making the already stifling night even more difficult to breathe in. Even when Toriano and several men came in with buckets of water to throw into the fire, and even when the firetrucks started coming, there was nothing more that anyone could do for Elena at that point.

The house, however, was saved. The only parts that were destroyed by the fire were the sealed-off back sala, and all the areas on the floors on top of it, which were made of wood. The wooden beams at the top of the wall of the second floor were also burnt, and so part of the roof there caved in, which gave the entire western wall a massive crack. This wall eventually toppled over at the force of the water from the fire trucks. By the time the fire was put out, the entire western part of the house at Hacienda Marianita was a gaping hole, while the rooms right next to the fire were left strangely untouched, the demarcation clearly visible as a neat, straight line, as if drawn with a pencil and straight-edge. Gone was the back sala, the corridor on the second floor that Assumpta knew was narrower than what it was supposed to be, the screened-in balcony on the second floor, Jacobo's office on the third floor that used to be Sebastian's, and Sebastian's bedroom on the fourth floor. The tower, and everything it used to hold, and everything below it as well, were gone.

Jacobo, true to form, lost no time in getting his house back in order. By dawn, men had already begun boarding up the entire western wall with sheets of plywood, which now was only two stories high once more, just as it was when Sebastian first built it. By the time the hardware stores were open in the town of Toog, Jacobo's business managers were there, ordering cement, hollow blocks, steel bars, and paint, to begin constructing a new western wall.

The rest of the house, undisturbed, managed to keep up the pretences of normalcy. In the centre of the foyer was the Christmas tree, an enormous fake white spruce, all bedecked in lights, red and green silk bows, paper poinsettias, large white trails of resin beads that were made to look like pearls, crystal balls tinted in different colours, and wooden toys in the shape of candy canes, reindeers, elves and cookies. There were also small box-shaped presents hung all over the tree, large red and plum-coloured berries made of glass, golden bells made of real metal and which rung like bells when they were nudged, and real pine cones. At the top of the tree was a star-shaped light made of crystal that was cut with various different mirrored facets, so that when the star was lit and the foyer lights dimmed, the entire foyer was swathed in shimmering bits of warm, golden light.

That Christmas tree and all of its ornaments were purchased by Margarita in Manila, during that one heady week in which she went there with Jacobo in 1948. Jacobo had to go to Intramuros for a business transaction and some legal matters, and Margarita, petulant and bored after having given birth to Paz only six weeks prior, insisted on going. They travelled via the Manila Railroad, which at that time was already mostly rebuilt after the war, and equipped with new diesel-powered trains. They stayed at the Manila Hotel, also newly rebuilt after the war, and while Jacobo dealt with business in Intramuros, Margarita explored the glinting displays of La Estrella del Norte, a massive department store in Escolta that sold everything from phonographs to jewellery to motor-cars. She was able to convince Jacobo to allow her to buy things for the house, so for the next few days of their stay in Manila, Margarita was at La Estrella every afternoon to go through fabrics for bed linens, drapes and upholstery, and chose what she thought would go well with the house. She also ordered new rugs for the library and the front sala, and new set of wood-and-iron seating for the lanai and the back garden. She ordered a small new chandelier for the foyer and three matching big ones for the ballroom.

But what she considered her best purchase was the Christmas tree, the whitish dusting on the top of the needles of the fake white spruce giving her the feel of an American Christmas. She had seen it on display in the centre of the department store, and had walked past it and around it several times, admiring the ornaments, before deciding to purchase the entire setup. The department store staff that she talked to did not even need ask Margarita if she was certain that the tree would fit inside her house, as everything she had purchased for the past few days was evidence enough that she owned a mansion, which the La Estrella itself was able to confirm when Margarita made the arrangements for them to transport her purchases to Camarines via the Manila Railroad.

The house at Hacienda Marianita already had a Christmas tree then, which had been placed on display in the foyer every December since 1935, but it looked too old-fashioned for Margarita, who had been inundated with modern posters about how a home should look like the entire time she was walking around La Estrella, and throwing away the old one in its entirety made complete sense to her. The only things from the old set that she held on to were the antique pewter picture frames that were traditionally hung on the lower branches of the tree to hold the individual portraits of children in the family that were twelve years old and younger, because the true identity of Santa Claus would not have been revealed to them yet at that age. Everyone in the house that was older than twelve was tasked to keep the magic of Christmas alive for people in the pewter picture frames, and it was a tradition that Margarita had been carrying and wanted to continue.

In 1957, the tree looked exactly the same as it had always looked starting in 1948, but this year, at the lowest of the branches, there hung only two of the antique pewter picture frames, holding the portraits of Paz, ten years old, and Assumpta, eight, but neither of them felt the magic of Christmas. Assumpta knew secrets that she should not, and Paz had absolutely no understanding of magic. Mercedes had not yet been found, either alive or in the form of a skeleton in the ashes left behind by the fire. And the rest of the people older than twelve were not faring any better.

In just a matter of a few days the house had a new western wall. It was a perfect replica of the old one in structure, design, and colour, except that the tower was gone, and even though that tower never really quite matched the rest of the house, now that it was gone, the Arguelleses, in their melancholy Christmas, wished it was still there.

Things were a lot different in the house at Hacienda Vida. The Monsantillos, naturally good-natured, managed to enjoy their Christmas. Salvador, half of his heart constantly gripped by fear regarding what could become of the hacienda, reserved the other half for the task of making sure his family never found this out, and his methods seemed to be effective. Consuela still had absolutely no idea.

After attending Christmas Mass on Christmas Eve at the parish church of Mangkono, they went back home to a *noche buena* meal with fish cocido, cochinilla, bibingka, and crema de fruita. There was a large quezo de bola at the centre of the dinner table, already cut up in thin slices with the red wax coating still on them. Bowls of fruit were arranged along the dinner table, carrying dalandan, bananas, mangoes, and little papayas. There was also kinunot, which was not a traditional dish for Christmas but was a special request of Beatriz, who was still too sick to go out of the house but was nevertheless awake for the first time in three weeks. She was carried downstairs to have noche buena with everyone else. She was pallid and thin, but noche buena at that time was a happy moment for her. Esperanza, less than three weeks into her spiteful marriage, also managed to laugh a little bit, and was temporarily nicer to her new husband and to her former friend Sofia.

That was when Beatriz Monsantillo would wake up for the very last time. On that Christmas Eve, while she slept, flowers began to grow on her bed and clothes, their roots white and as fine as hair that could weave through the fibres of the fabric, getting their nourishment from Beatriz's very essence, not so much drinking her in but expanding her, waking up for her, growing from tendril to bud to full bloom on behalf of her.

Chapter 12

Hills of Sound

It was Yaya Lina who heard the first name that the sleeping Beatriz uttered, two weeks after she had stopped waking up. She had just finished wiping Beatriz's arms with a damp wash cloth, carefully avoiding the cannula on her left hand. The intravenous medication had been installed in the bedroom after the doctors that were called to the house could not wake Beatriz up. However, as her vital signs were stable, she had no history of seizures, heart attacks, or any allergic shocks, they could not foresee any future medical emergency, so they declared that Beatriz was in a coma and let her stay in her bedroom. A nurse was sent from the hospital in the town centre every four hours to check her vital signs, to replenish her intravenous medication as it ran out, and to admire the new flowers that came out from the bed linens that day.

Nuns from the Colegio de Santa Rita also came regularly to pray the rosary around Beatriz's bed, with Yaya Lina standing watch, making sure the nuns don't utter their Ave Marias too loudly. After their prayers they would touch the flowers and admire them, but because there were no roses, they looked a little disappointed, as roses were the signature flower of Santa Maria, and the reason why the santisimo rosario was named such. Each time they returned, they would very discreetly look for rosebuds, their faces looking hopeful, and each time they didn't see the rosebuds their faces would fall, ever so slightly. Consuela and Salvador and sometimes the children would drop in a few times during the day, but it was Yaya Lina who stayed with Beatriz round the clock. By this time, she had already memorized the number, colours and placement of all the flowers that had grown, so she could tell which ones were new.

She had already begun brushing Beatriz's hair, spread out on the pillow, as best as she could, because of the flowers that were growing through it, when she noticed two new buds growing near the corner of the pillowcase, where the night before there were none there.

'Magdalena,' Beatriz said softly.

'What?' Yaya Lina stopped what she was doing and looked at the girl's face.

Beatriz was silent, except for the sound of her deep and even breathing.

Yaya Lina placed her ear right next the Beatriz's mouth and waited for several seconds.

'Juana,' Beatriz said.

'Ay!' Yaya Lina jumped back. 'Did you hear that?' she said to Bituin, the maid who was sweeping the floor of Beatriz's room.

'Hear what?'

'What Beatriz said?'

'No. What did she say?' Bituin said, walking over to Beatriz, still holding the broom.

'She said Magdalena, and then Juana.'

'I didn't hear anything.'

Then they both stared at Beatriz, leaning in, waiting for her to speak again.

After several minutes, Beatriz said, 'Narcisa.'

'Ay!' Yaya Lina said again, covering her mouth, while Bituin dropped her broom. They stayed there, transfixed.

'Leonor,' Beatriz said.

'She might be waking up. Go get Doña Consuela, now! Go!' Yaya Lina told Bituin, who promptly ran out to find her. While waiting, Yaya Lina ran to Beatriz's little desk by the window, took a pencil and a sheet of paper from Beatriz's notebook, and wrote down the names she heard Beatriz say. She could only remember the last and the first and the second, but could not remember the others.

As for Bituin, that very same day she asked the majordoma never to make her enter Beatriz's bedroom again, because she remembered the sad lady wearing blue that looked like Beatriz and who was always standing by the windows of the house at Hacienda Vida, the one that Beatriz once told her was sewing a very large quilt made of names.

Consuela, on the other hand, regarded that as a sign that the doctors must be summoned once again upon the onset of this new symptom, and they did come, but they still could not get Beatriz to wake up. However, her vital signs were stable, and they could find nothing medically wrong with her, so they continued with the current treatment plan, which was to ignore the flowers while feeding her with Dextrose, and nothing more. The nuns came more frequently, braving the extremely hot weather in the open vehicle of Colegio de Santa Rita, their faces looking even more hopeful as they glanced across the bed of flowers on Beatriz's bed and nightgown, looking for rosebuds.

As the days went by, Beatriz mentioned more names, a few each day, and Yaya Lina listed them all down on the pieces of paper as she heard them. She was so diligent in this task that no one had asked her to do, but that she felt was somehow important. Most of the time she was so bent on looking at Beatriz's face, waiting for her to speak a name, that she never noticed the few times when a lady in blue that looked like Beatriz was standing by Beatriz's window, also listening for names.

The people of Camarines tried to live their days out as normally as possible despite the ongoing drought, so the days in the town of Toog were still quite bustling, but the nights were terribly still and quiet, as if the heat had sucked up all animation that could come from the living things remaining alive. Everyone felt lethargic, preferring not to move or even speak under the weight of the oppressive heat.

But that night, in bed beside Apolonio in his small cottage, Filomena spoke.

'The hills will walk to the house at Hacienda Marianita,' she said, 'and then the sea will walk to the land.'

Apolonio, only half-asleep because of heat exhaustion, looked at Filomena and thought she was the most beautiful woman he had ever seen.

Jacobo decided to abandon the search for Mercedes two months after the fire. None of her remains have been found in the rubble of the western wall of the house at Hacienda Marianita when the workers were building the new wall, and the Chief of Police of the town of Toog had come up with nothing, just as he had not come up with anything much with the other previous investigations on the things that had happened in the house. Nevertheless, Jacobo could not be completely irate with him, as he had been quite effective at very kindly providing other things for him that were outside the purview of the law. Of course he was also paying him a princely sum every month for that specific kindness, but Jacobo was not worried at all that the Chief of Police had information about him that could potentially undo every progress he had made with the hacienda over the years, because in the very decision that he had made to fulfil Jacobo's requests, he had already implicated himself into the schemes. There was no way for the Chief of Police to bring him down without bringing destruction on himself.

The negotiations with the workers had finally failed, as Jacobo continued to insist on keeping the same wages instead of giving in to the repeated requests over the years to raise them. Jacobo considered the failure of negotiations a victory for the hacienda, but for some reason, he could not shake the memory of the multong vengativa out of his head. He tried to reason the ghost away, telling himself that no one, much less this ghost, had any grounds for exacting vengeance on him for he had murdered no one, had killed only in self-defence, and was even providing means for these people to stay alive even in this drought. Regardless of the status of each harvest, his workers were consistently paid, their housing and medical needs provided for. Jacobo, in his propensity to not pay any attention to the past, and compounded by the Arguelleses's complete lack of habit to document anything, was not aware that the true problem was not his workers but the descendants of the people that the three families had robbed of their land many years ago. He had never looked at the maps of Camarines in the library, never paid any attention to how each map had become different over the years. Because of this, Jacobo lacked not just the information but also the insight, and this was how the Chief of Police, who knew about the disenfranchisement, had eventually failed Jacobo. The Chief of Police had always known the root cause of what had been going on, knew about the infection that had been festering for decades, but did nothing beyond keeping the status quo for the man who had him in his pocket.

It should already be the end of what was normally considered summer, but there had been no hint of rain for a very long time. In the utter lack of wind and rain, the night was very still in Toog, so every single sound carried across the open air. Guadalupe, whose hearing had become even stronger and sharper over time, was just about to sleep, because she had to wait for the entire grounds to be completely quiet. The clock on her night stand said it was two o'clock in the morning, and the last clear sound she heard was two of Jacobo's bodyguards acknowledging each other as they met while making their rounds around the house.

'Jesucristo, this heat!' one bodyguard said.

The other guard laughed. 'You're only feeling hot because you've had some gin to drink earlier.'

'I did not.' More laughter, then Guadalupe heard them walk on.

She could also hear Pato, the head guard, saying something, but he was too far away, in the main driveway, for her to really hear what he was saying. Then Paz walked past her bed from the smaller bedroom inside Guadalupe's and left the room, closing the door behind her. Guadalupe heard Paz's footsteps fading down the corridor. After these sounds had finally died down, she closed her eyes, and began thinking her nighttime prayers. She no longer voiced them out, as the sound of her own voice had become too much for her ears.

Then she started hearing different sounds, softly, and as if from far away, much farther than where Pato was. She opened her eyes again, training her ears on where she thought the sound was coming from. They were coming from the southern part of the house, where Mercedes's windows faced, towards the rolling hills of the hacienda. After a very short while the sounds became closer, and Guadalupe could make out that they sounded like leaves and twigs, rustling, as if there was a breeze, as if they were coming closer. Guadalupe felt no breeze inside her bedroom despite the wide open windows, but she thought maybe there was a breeze outside, and dismissed the sound.

Assumpta was in her secret room until very late that night, making more complicated versions of the new maps of the house she had drawn, after the western wall had been rebuilt. She had already gotten used to her new kind of eyesight. Her right eye had gone completely blind, but the eyesight in her left eye had become very sharp. The doctor in the town centre had given her an eye patch so that she would not have to see anything as double images, one image a blurred, ghostly twin attached to the clear, actual object or person. Assumpta liked the eye patch. It made her feel like she was an aged, experienced cartographer, her body ravaged by the years she had spent riding the galleon ships to explore the world and draw the maps of what she had found, little by little changing them from the old maps with unknown areas whose spaces were marked with drawings of beasts and monsters, to new maps that showed what land was actually there. But since she could not even leave the house, let alone become a cartographer travelling the world in a galleon ship, she drew new maps of the house instead.

That was what she was doing until very late that night. When she got sleepy, she placed all the papers into the old briefcase and laid the briefcase inside the bathtub, and then she left the room and went upstairs to go to bed. The house was very faintly heaving, and to Assumpta it felt rhythmic, as if the house was breathing, but she had already gotten used to it by then. As she was passing by one of the windows on the second floor, in the corridor near Mercedes's bedroom, she saw, from the corner of her one good eye, a movement outside. She stepped up to the window, and in the darkness, she could see small hills moving very slowly towards the house, bringing with them a slight rustling sound like leaves and twigs in the breeze. She closed her eyes and shook her head, doubting her own vision for a moment, but when she looked again, the hills were unmistakably there, creeping forward almost unnoticeably. The moon was high and large in the sky, so the grounds outside were illuminated by a silver glow. Deep inside the hills that were closest to the house, she saw human eyes looking out. She started backing away from the window, as quietly as she could, and ran to Margarita's bedroom.

'Mama,' she said and shook Margarita, who was deeply asleep with a sleep mask made of silk over her eyes.

Margarita groaned and took off her sleep mask. 'Assumpta, what are you doing?'

'Be quiet, Mama,' Assumpta whispered, 'the hills are coming.'

'What? What hills? *Que pasando?*'

'We have to hide, Mama,' said Assumpta, pulling her mother out of bed.

'Assumpta, tell me right now, que esta pasando.' Margarita's voice was louder as she started to feel more awake. '*Contesta* me!'

'Shh!' Assumpta hissed at her, and pulled her along. 'We must get the others. Walk lightly, Mama.'

Margarita let out a sigh and allowed herself to be pulled into Jacobo II's bedroom, which was right next to hers.

Assumpta poked Jacobo II on the arm until he woke up, and she pulled him out of bed. 'We must hide. Hurry. We need to get the others.'

Jacobo II rolled out of bed, 'Que pasando? Where's Papa?'

'Shh! We'll get him next,' Assumpta said.

'Assumpta, por dios y por santo,' Margarita began to say, but then they heard gunshots from outside the house. The room nearest to them was Guadalupe's and they barged in, but she wasn't there. Assumpta ran further inside to the bedroom she shared with Paz, but Paz was not there.

She ran out the room and across the corridor to barge into Mrs Palacio's bedroom. The old woman was already sitting upright in her bed, pale and trembling.

'*Vamos!*' Margarita ordered.

Assumpta ran to Mrs Palacio, grabbed her arm and dragged her out of bed.

They heard more gunshots from outside, and knew she had to move fast. 'Follow me!' she said, no longer needing to whisper.

'I'll get Papa,' Jacobo II said.

'There is no time!' Assumpta screamed at him. 'He has a gun, we do not.'

She pulled Jacobo II's arm and ran to the stairs, with Margarita close behind them, and when they got to the middle landing, Assumpta pushed the secret panel aside.

'Go in and go down the stairs,' she whispered. 'Quickly.'

Assumpta made Margarita crawl in first, followed by Mrs Palacio, then Jacobo II next. Assumpta crawled through last, putting the panel back into place behind her. Then they all went down the stairs and entered Assumpta's secret room with the claw-foot bathtub. Assumpta kept the overhead light turned off, but they could still see each other inside the room, the moonlight powerful enough to shine through the small windows that were facing the stables. They looked at each other, not saying anything. Assumpta wondered where Paz was, Jacobo II wondered where Inez was, Mrs Palacio had her eyes shut tight, praying for the safety of everyone in the house, and Margarita fervently tried to make herself feel guilty at not making an effort to get her husband, but failing to feel the guilt. A few moments later they heard a big crash, and they all knew that none of them could do anything.

But Inez was in a different situation. When she heard the first gunshots from her bedroom, she woke up and ran to her window, which was facing east. Down below she saw men disguised as shrubbery, long rifles pointed at three of Jacobo's guards stationed at the main door. Inez took her sheathed bolo from under her bed, tied it to her waist, and ran out of her bedroom. She barged into Jacobo II's bedroom, but he was no longer there, the three being in Paz's bedroom at that very same moment. She ran to the next bedroom, which was Jacobo's, and saw that he was just getting out of bed.

'Papa, there are men with guns outside,' she said calmly.

Jacobo took his revolver from the drawer in his night stand. 'Go back inside your bedroom and hide,' he told Inez.

Inez had no plans to obey her father's orders. She left his room, but not to return to hers. Instead, she ran towards the stairs, barging into Guadalupe's room on the way, but Guadalupe wasn't there. She ran further in to get Paz and Assumpta, but the room was empty. She then decided to go to Margarita's room, but when she turned the corner, she saw her father just going in, so she ran to the stairs instead.

By the time she reached the top landing, the secret panel had just been shut closed by Assumpta. She ran down to the foyer, hid behind a very tall vase, and heard the main door crash open. From where she was hiding she saw some of the intruders, still clad in shrubbery, run up the stairs, shouting Jacobo's name. They were fast, but Inez could see that only two of them were carrying rifles. Unafraid and running on adrenaline, she unsheathed her bolo and ran out the door, and met two more men with shrubbery on their heads, and by instinct, she slashed the stomach of the one nearest her, who fell to the floor with a strong grunt. The other man tried to swing at her with his bolo but she crouched and hacked him on the leg. He screamed, but one of Jacobo's bodyguards walked in carrying a rifle, shot the screaming man, and then ran upstairs. Inez heard the sound of gunshots upstairs, and she walked out of the main door, prepared to hack more intruders.

One of Jacobo's bodyguards was on the señorita steps, wounded. 'Señorita!' he called out to her. 'Don't go out there.'

Inez ignored him and continued walking, staying close to the wall of the house. As she neared the corner that led to the north wall, she met another intruder and hacked him on the neck. He was closely followed by another man who charged at Inez, but she crouched again and swung her bolo around, cutting him on the lower legs. As he lay on the ground screaming, Inez stood over him and slashed him on the chest once, which made the screaming stop. Inez felt the rush of her first kills surge through her veins. Then Toriano and some men from the stables came running around the corner, saw Inez, a bolo in her hand and her clothes covered in blood, and they stopped in their tracks.

'Señorita, are you hurt?' Toriano said, coming closer.

'I'm fine. The bastards are upstairs. Go. Look for Mama and my sisters,' Inez said, and then walked to the stables, more of her father's men rushing past her with their own bolos. When she got there, she saddled a steed and rode off to get Pato, the head guard, who was most likely near the main gate, which was to the east. She figured the intruders most likely entered the grounds from the southwest, which was the least guarded side because that was the side closest to the rolling hills, which were supposed to be a natural barrier against intruders, but tonight, it seemed that the hills themselves that were supposed to guard the Arguelleses had come to the house at Hacienda Marianita.

Inez sped forward, and along the way, she saw men who had fallen, some of them wearing shrubbery, and some of them recognizable to her as Pato's men. In the light of the full moon, their blood looked black on the closely trimmed grass. Inez realized that Pato already knew about the intruders and had sent his men to the house, but she still wanted to find him. He had to help her go back to the house with armed men so she could look for her mother and sisters. She knew her father and her brother would be able to defend themselves, but the women, she knew, were fair game to the *cabrones* who invaded her house. She was not very much afraid for herself, but she was terrified for them.

Even before the hills entered the house, Guadalupe, who could not sleep because of all the rustling that she had been trying to ignore, walked out of her bedroom and walked to the new lounge at western side of the house, which Jacobo had built after the fire. There she saw Paz, standing by the window that was facing west.

'Do you hear that?' Guadalupe asked sitting on the chair nearest Paz.

'Hear what?'

'The rustling.'

'I don't hear anything,' Paz said, looking out the window with her elbows on the sill. 'I came here because it was too hot in my room.'

'Where is Assumpta?'

'I don't know. I haven't seen her all night.'

Guadalupe was quiet for a moment, and then she started hearing male voices from the other side of the house. She knew Paz could not hear them, but when she heard gunshots, she blurted out, 'Now do you hear it?'

'Yes, yes I heard it!' Paz said, whipping around to face the room.

Guadalupe heard people running, Assumpta whispering, and the voices of Margarita and Jacobo II, and even more running, doors opening and closing, all on the second floor, and then moving on down the stairs. All the while, Paz was still standing by the window, paralysed, looking at Guadalupe with big eyes.

When they both heard the main door crash open, Guadalupe pulled Paz down to the floor, and they crawled to hide behind the long sofa, holding each other's hand.

'What's going on?' Paz whispered.

'I don't know,' Guadalupe said, but she trained her ears once more to the sound, trying to figure out what was happening, and where everyone was. In the cacophony of gunshots and shouts and running, she could not identify anyone, but when she tried harder she heard Inez breathing from the foyer at the first floor, and she felt grateful that at least another sister was alive. She trained her ears on Inez, following her sound, so she knew when Inez killed at least three men, and told someone to go find her mother and sisters. Guadalupe closed her eyes and prayed the 'Ave Maria', pleading for the help sent by Inez to find her and Paz soon, but then two more gunshots were fired right on the second floor, the sound explosive in Guadalupe's ears, and Paz shuddered, grunted loudly, and fell sideways into her arms. At the same moment, Guadalupe felt the floor under her heave heavily, and her first thought was that Paz felt it and was reacting to it.

'Ssssshhh…' Guadalupe told her sister. 'It's all right. Inez sent help. Help is on the way.'

But Paz did not reply, and Guadalupe felt a warm liquid trickling down her hands. Around them, the house continued to heave.

Guadalupe and Paz were found before dawn, still behind the sofa. By that time, Paz's blood had become sticky and tacky in Guadalupe's hands, and it had trickled down, slow and thick, along her arms and dripped from her elbows, but she did not want to move and did not even open her eyes. She opened them only when she heard people calling out their names.

By dawn, Jacobo had a clear idea of what had happened. Men, who lived near the coast of Toog, their families relegated there decades ago when Sebastian built Hacienda Marianita, had been planning for years to kill Jacobo. Their first plan was to assassinate him quietly in bed as he slept but that plan failed, and their second plan to burn the entire house, with the Arguelleses inside it, failed as well. Their third attempt to kill Jacobo, which had to include overpowering the entire house on account of the new bodyguards, had also failed, as Jacobo had survived the invasion. He had even killed two of his would-be assassins, and the bodyguard, who ran upstairs after killing the man Inez had hacked downstairs, managed to kill another. Together, Jacobo and the bodyguard were able to run into Guadalupe's bedroom, and barricaded themselves inside by quickly pushing her heavy bed against the door that had no lock on it. Then they went back further into the inner bedroom of Paz and Assumpta, whose door had no lock on it either, and pushed the two beds against the door. The rest of the invaders, carrying bolos, tried hacking Guadalupe's door open, but Toriano and the men from the stables came and overpowered them, Toriano getting his arm hacked after killing one intruder by hacking him on the neck. The remaining intruders scampered away, but on their way out, they were intercepted by a group of approaching policemen, their service firearms drawn, who were called by one of Pato's men who had rushed to the police precinct on a bicycle the moment Pato sensed that something was wrong in the house.

Paz died in the arms of Guadalupe in the small hours of the morning of that day. When they were found behind the sofa, the policemen didn't even bother to revive Paz, as she had already bled out profusely, the bullet cutting cleanly through the back of the sofa, tearing through Paz's small back at an oblique angle, and exiting straight through her heart, finally going through a wooden panel below the window sill where, only hours ago, Paz had been resting her elbows looking out into the hot night. She died instantly, which nevertheless was no comfort to anyone. Jacobo was thoroughly enraged, and threw an armchair into a wooden wall, splitting the wall into two. Margarita was inconsolable, part of her hating Jacobo for not protecting their daughter, and another part of her hating herself for not doing the same thing. And Guadalupe, her sister's blood all over her, walked quietly to her bedroom, past her bed that was askew on the floor, past the beds of Assumpta and the now-dead Paz in the inner bedroom, into the bathroom that they all shared, took off her bloody dress, and cradled it in her arms while she cried, cried like she had never cried before. She cried for Paz who died afraid, cried for Mercedes who had disappeared and had never been found, cried for Marianita who was killed by Sebastian in the bathroom when he pushed her and she fell and hit her head on the corner of the sink, Marianita who tried to send letters to her own mother to let her know how Sebastian had been treating her, but whose every effort to get the word out had been blocked by her husband. Outside the bathroom where Guadalupe cried, the house at Hacienda Marianita was in total disarray, the floors bloody and strewn with mud and leaves and twigs, the furniture thrown about, the drapes torn. Policemen were walking around, documenting the destruction and carting off corpses, not noticing the house heaving under their boot-clad feet. And while Guadalupe cried, cradling her sister's blood, rain suddenly began to fall strongly over all of Camarines. Agua de Mayo had finally arrived, and it ended the drought that had been going on for almost a year.

Chapter 13

The Women

The Agua de Mayo that ended the drought in Camarines fell steadily for seven days. Within the first several minutes, it had washed the blood off the grass on the grounds around the house at Hacienda Marianita, rainwater bringing the blood deep into the soil below. After a few hours, the grounds were completely soaked, the flowers sodden in the flowerbeds, and the perfectly manicured shrubbery drooping under the weight of the raindrops. The police vehicles coming in and out of the grounds created muddy trails on the grass and created dips where they parked for longer than a few minutes. On the next morning of the downpour, the drainage system in the town centre of Toog began to overflow, flooding the streets with two inches of water, flotsam accumulating in street corners where the eddies formed. By the end of the second day, the town centre of Toog was ankle-deep in rainwater. In Mangkono, Salvador's fish pens had overflown with water, which did not really matter to him, as they had all been empty for months since the massive fish kill.

When the policemen were finally done trooping in and out of the house at Hacienda Marianita, the Arguelleses shut their doors and windows against the wet darkness outside, had the maids clean up the whole house, and began the private wake for Paz. Two men from the funeral home had brought in the casket, white and small, with Paz inside, nestled in the peach-coloured silk lining. They were the same people who had brought Paz away on the morning that she died, for an official autopsy and then for embalming. Paz had now returned to her home, wearing her favourite white dress made of an eyelet fabric, with puffed sleeves, a tight square neckline, a wide silk ribbon at the waist, a full skirt with big pockets, and a hem that reached her calves. On her feet were white socks trimmed with white lace and white shoes made of patent leather, which Paz used to wear when she went to church with the family on Sunday mornings. After the men from the funeral home had set the casket on its stand in the middle of the living room on the first floor, Margarita went to Paz, touched her face gently, smoothed the black, curly hair over her forehead, touched her arms that were crossed over her chest, and tucked Paz's rosary, in use only for about two years, under her small fingers. Then she whispered, 'Adios, mi amor,' and as she watched the people from the funeral home carefully placing the glass sheet over the open casket, she wondered if Paz had heard her over the sound of the rain.

Guadalupe could, from her bedroom on the second floor. When she heard the people from the funeral home arriving, she went to her closet and took out her dress, still soaked and now stiff with Paz's blood, which she had been hiding wrapped in a bed sheet. She had been unsure whether to wash it, unsure whether she should keep a physical memory of Paz dying, but upon hearing her mother say goodbye to her sister, she knew she herself could never say goodbye to Paz, so she put the bloody dress back in its special hiding place. This would be her own version of Marianita's letters, except that what was done to Paz was no secret.

The weather reports published in the local newspapers and broadcast over the local radio stations reported no typhoon over

Camarines, just rains. And the rain, indeed, did not look like a typhoon. There was no thunder or lightning or wind. There was just rain, nothing but rain, falling incessantly, with large, heavy raindrops that landed on the roofs of houses and buildings and which burst into much smaller droplets to splash further downwards. The raindrops that fell directly into the ever-rising flood made splashes, so that there were big drops falling down, and tiny drops going upwards. The 102-year-old Mrs Epifania Reyes, who had never experienced a drought her entire life that she had lived in Camarines, had concluded that she had also hitherto never experienced such an interminable Agua de Mayo. Her great-grandchildren had to carry her to the second floor of her house because water had begun to enter the first floor.

On the fourth day of the downpour, the Visbales in the house at Hacienda Dolores began complaining of the wet, dark weather, which they normally preferred. Their house was ensconced within a thick grove of trees, and the sound there of the incessant rain was thunderous. Rain fell heavily on the tree canopies, making each leaf droop and act as a slide on which the water flowed down. Instead of hearing a mass of individual raindrops falling on their roof made of mosaic tiles, the Visbales heard an entire blanket of dripping water, compounded by the sound of rain falling on the trees above their roof, and the sound of the raindrops falling on the knee-deep flood that was covering the grounds around the house. This combination of sounds, which had been going on for days, made them go slightly unhinged. Selina Suarez had not left her suite of rooms since her husband and second cousin Pacifico Visbal died laughing, but on the fourth day of the downpour she opened her door, emerged from her room, walked out of the house, and into the flood. In the rest of Camarines, no land remained uncovered by the flood except for the rolling hills. There was water over the towns, over the barangays, over the fish farm, over the rice and abaca plantations. There was water inside the first floor of houses and stores, water in the schools and offices, water in the streets and highways and open, unused land, all the way to the coastline of Camarines, where on the sixth day, the flood, composed of rainwater, finally met the saltwater of the swollen sea, forming a seamless blanket of water as far as the eyes could see.

Two minutes after midnight on the seventh day, the rain stopped as suddenly as it had started. Many of the people of Camarines, who, to some degree, had already begun getting accustomed to the sound, were still up that late, their usual sleeping habits disrupted by the sound and the cold and the dampness. They had also become accustomed to speaking slightly louder than normal, in order to be heard over the sound of the downpour, so when the rain abruptly stopped, many people were caught half-shouting, startled into stopping in mid-sentence by the complete and sudden absence of thrumming. When dawn arrived, people could actually see the sun in the sky, a weak yellow blob behind light grey clouds that eventually disappeared towards noon, allowing the sun to display itself in full.

The flood took three days to subside completely, and left everything muddy and strewn with pieces of garbage. The people of Toog embarked on a major cleanup, starting with their own homes and shops, and then eventually spanning out to clean the streets. Luningning herself lost no time in organizing the servants of the house at Hacienda Marianita into their own cleanup of the grounds. The gardeners came in bearing wheelbarrows of garden soil and mulch, and they fixed the flower beds, levelled the soil under the shaped hedges, and cleared the grass of loose leaves and branches. The garden walkways, the tiled pavement surrounding the house, the stone señorita steps leading to the main house, and the entire lower wall of the house were scrubbed clean of mud. The driveway was refilled with gravel after the flood washed most of it away. By the time the servants were done, the house exterior and its grounds looked beautiful and polished once more, and gleamed as if nothing terrible had just happened, as if somewhere in the grass on the western part of the grounds, there did not nestle a bullet that claimed a small girl's life. And while everyone in Camarines worked to put their houses back in order, one of the guards of the house at Hacienda Dolores, who was riding on horseback along the wide creek that ran along the edge of the house grounds, found the lifeless, black-clad body of Selina along its bank. Had her body not been found that day, none of her relatives would have known that she had already died.

Jacobo did not let Paz's death go easily. Several times a day, he doggedly hounded the Chief of Police to conclude the investigation on the invasion of his home, so that the remaining men who had been caught could be tried and then thrown into jail, their confessions used to find the mastermind of the entire plot. In the beginning, Jacobo would use the telephone; then when he suspected that the Chief of Police had been trying to avoid his intrusive phone calls, he became even more intrusive by dropping in at his office in the town centre during random hours of the day. All of the intruders that were caught had been identified, but beyond admitting to being at the house, they would admit to nothing else, which infuriated Jacobo to no end. He wanted to know who was heading these plans to destroy him and his family, so he could have them thrown in jail as well, never to bother him again, at least that was what he told the Chief of Police. He might be dangerous, but his danger was precise, and he did not want to murder anyone who did not need to be. In his relentless pursuit of this specific information so that he could be righteous in his planned murder, right after hiring additional bodyguards and assigning them to his wife and children, he ignored his grieving family, even Jacobo II, to whom he had begun to delegate more of the administrative work of the hacienda. He had expressed no sadness and had never been seen crying. Instead, his face developed a dark and hardened look, as if he was eternally cross. No one could talk to him about anything other than matters connected to the hacienda. He had even stopped having dinner with his family, instead having dinner brought to his office every night before retiring to bed. In his seemingly outright and deliberate neglect of the emotional needs of his family, Margarita had sworn that Jacobo no longer existed to her.

When Assumpta emerged from the secret room with her mother and her brother and Mrs Palacio into a house in complete chaos, she felt ridiculous and realized that Paz was right in thinking her maps were crazy. A few days later, she returned to her secret room, actually no longer a secret, to cut up every single sheet of paper she had inside the old briefcase with the biggest pair of shears she could find in the house. She could see no point in drawing further maps of the house, and no point in keeping what she had already drawn. With pursed lips and one good eye, she sat on the floor of her secret room and snipped papers into small pieces, every single one of them, including Sebastian's papers, which were so thin and brittle that they had a crinkling sound when she snipped them. As she snipped, she tried to feel the house heaving, but felt nothing; what she did feel was the shrinking of all her memories, of her time spent in the library reading and going through the old maps, time spent exploring the house, time spent ruminating, time spent making these very same drawings that she was now destroying. With every snip, a memory shrunk into a tiny, dense ball of charcoal in her heart. When all of the paper sheets have been turned into very small pieces, she placed every single piece back into the briefcase. She felt inside one of the elasticated pockets of the briefcase where she had been keeping Sebastian's key since the day she found it, and wondered how she could cut that into small pieces, but she suddenly lost interest in the whole enterprise, closed the briefcase, placed it inside the bathtub, walked out the door, no longer eight but much older.

A month after the two burials, one day, bright and clear, as if the deluge and the deaths never happened, Yaya Lina was in Beatriz's room, tending to the sleeping girl as she has done for the past few months. She smoothed down Beatriz's night gown as best as she could, because the flowers on the bedsheets had also begun growing on the night gown, but as Beatriz never moved, there was almost nothing to smooth down. She wiped Beatriz's face with a washcloth dampened with warm water from a basin and also brushed the girl's hair that was spread out over the pillow as best as she could, for there were flowers sprouting from there as well. Then Yaya Lina put away the brush, and used her fat, wrinkled hands to smooth down the child's hair, interspersed with the fine, hair-like tendrils of the roots of the flowers. She could tell them apart only because the flowers' roots were white, like Beatriz's bed linens, while Beatriz's hair was a deep black. Her hair looked neither like Monsantillo hair, which was straight and medium brown, nor Visbal hair, which was blonde and wiry. She was the only Monsantillo daughter that had Arguelles hair, curly and shiny and black, which was always loose around her shoulders, and which bounced and glimmered in the sunlight when she played outside. Yaya Lina looked at Beatriz for several more minutes, watching her chest rise rhythmically in long, deep breaths, waiting for her to utter a name, but heard none. The uttering of the name happened less and less now. Her list had not had a new name for the past four days. Then Yaya Lina took the washcloth and the basin, and stepped out of the bedroom to bring them to the laundress, but right after she stepped out,

Beatriz uttered one final name, a name that Yaya Lina would not be able to write on her list of names.

Yaya Lina went back to Beatriz's room right away but did not notice anything different. She went to her armchair beside the girl's bed, sat down and resumed reading *An Pagcabuhay Can Manga Santo*, the Bicol version of *The Lives of the Saints*. She was on the part about Santa Teresa de Avila, a Spanish socialite who decided to become a nun and then became famous for her rapturous episodes in which she was said to have levitated while rose petals fell from the skies to the ground around her. Her corpse was also said to be incorruptible, but as was the habit of the Roman Catholic Church that valued display over true preservation, the saint was taken out of her coffin, her arm hacked off in order to be placed in a reliquary for the faithful to pray to, and only after all that was the rest of her body interred. Yaya Lina buried herself in her reading, almost smelling the roses being described in the book, and heard Beatriz laugh, quite loudly.

Yaya Lina's heart stopped, she dropped her book on her lap, and her head snapped to look at Beatriz, who was as unmoving as she had been for the past several weeks, ensconced in her bed and the flowers. The laugher came again, sounding undeniably like Beatriz, but this time from Yaya Lina's other side, so she looked there but saw no one. Her heart started beating again, but slowly, and with a tremendous pounding that felt almost like it was going to choke her. She looked slowly around the room, waiting for Beatriz to laugh again and was still for an interminable moment until it dawned on her that Beatriz was already dead. She bolted up from her seat, her book falling to the floor, and, terrified, she went to Beatriz's body and put her ear right in front of Beatriz's mouth, trying to listen to her breathing, and, hopefully, a name, but she heard nothing even after several minutes. Then she placed a hand on the girl's chest.

There was no heart beating there. She pulled her hand away and watched for the rising and falling of the chest, saw none, and ran out of the room, trampling over *An Pagcabuhay Kan Manga Santo*, screaming, 'Doña Consuela! Doña Consuela!'

At that very same moment, Salvador was sitting across the table from Jacobo, in Jacobo's new office on the first floor of the house at Hacienda Marianita, and he felt a twinge in his chest, a tiny one, but he must have winced nevertheless.

'Are you okay, compadre?' Jacobo asked.

'I'm fine,' said Salvador, thinking of San Benito. 'I just haven't been sleeping well lately.'

'Well, you can start sleeping well again now. Your problems will be held at bay until you find a long-term solution.'

'Gracias, compadre,' said Salvador, sincerely, for Jacobo has been truly generous.

Salvador has been losing money steadily while the rot inexplicably continued in his abaca storages, despite the procurement and installation of new and more modern dehumidifiers. His fish farm in Labo had not recovered yet from the long drought, despite the seven-day Agua de Mayo that ended it. He did not want to bother Jacobo at first, who was still in mourning after the death of Paz and whose remaining problems, he heard, were just as massive, and even potentially illegal, but Salvador was at the end of his rope. For the sake of his family, he had to get help, and Jacobo was the most natural source of help he could think of. The Visbales had become more cloistered than ever after the death of Pacifico and then of Selina, and Salvador did not even know how to approach them to begin with, but with Jacobo now being his compadre, he felt there would be more understanding.

And there was. Jacobo, albeit dark and unsmiling, proved to be sympathetic about the expensive upkeep of the house at Hacienda Vida, which included the medical expenses of

Beatriz who had, until then, remained undiagnosed. At the thought of Beatriz, Salvador felt another twinge in his chest, this time a little stronger, and there was an ominousness to it.

'Ah!' Salvador said, now feeling a strong urge to go home. 'I must go. I must check on the house.'

'Esta bien,' Jacobo said, and then added, 'How is Beatriz?'

'She is still the same, compadre. No change at all.'

'Ah,' Jacobo said, looking thoughtful, barely noticing that Salvador was turning slightly green. 'Anyway, let me know if there is anything else I can do for you, compadre.' He stood from his seat and walked over to Salvador to shake his hand.

'Of course, compadre,' said Salvador, trying to make his handshake grip strong. 'But this is already too much, and I am eternally grateful for the help.' He meant what he said.

Salvador thought that Jacobo seemed to bounce back well from all of his problems, but of course he knew nothing of the full extent of the complications in Hacienda Marianita. All he could see was what was on the surface. Jacobo's house, this very same one that had been razed by fire only months ago, invaded later by armed assassins, and in which Paz was killed, had been restored in record time. All walls that had bullet holes and hack marks from bolos were either patched up and painted over or replaced entirely. Guadalupe's bedroom got an entirely new door. Sebastian's old tower that contained his bedroom, and Marianita's back sala, sealed against time for decades, had been destroyed in the fire from December. In the place of the back sala, Jacobo had a new office built, and this new office had a much more modern design than the rest of the house, yet another transmogrification, a departure from what was originally intended. Another transmogrification was that the lounge on the second floor on the side facing west, just installed after the fire to replace part of the screened-in balcony, was walled up and sealed off. This was Jacobo's decision, because he wanted no one to ever walk into the space where Paz had died.

The entire household was in the traditional state of mourning, with everyone, including the servants, wearing all black, and refraining from attending social gatherings. This would be the norm for an entire year. Margarita, however, would wear black for the rest of her life and would never leave the house again. She moved into Mercedes's old bedroom, which was farthest from Jacobo's, to make it easier for her to avoid seeing her husband.

In his Berlina motor-car on the way to his house in Mangkono, Salvador felt like he would vomit with heavy fear, yet he did not ask Busoy to drive faster, because he knew that would make no difference, not to Busoy's driving speed, not to his escalating feeling of being ill, and certainly not to what he felt was going on in his house that he could not understand. He knew that he had done the last of what he could do when he asked for Jacobo's help, in his one last attempt to twist the hand of destiny, and he did not even know how that would turn out. That decision of his could prove to be wrong somewhere along the way, but from here on out, he was utterly powerless over what was bound to happen, and so was San Benito's oracion in keeping out the incoming darkness. The best that Salvador could do was to refuse to drink the proverbial poison.

When he got to the house at Hacienda Vida, Consuela came running out to meet him in the foyer, distraught, her eyes all red, her arms flying.

'Your daughter is dead!' Consuela called out even before she had reached him and had fallen into his arms. But then she felt bile rising up her throat; she knew she had to correct what she had said.

'Beatriz is dead,' Consuela whispered into her husband's chest, and Salvador, who, for several months, had been on the verge of a dark pit, felt himself finally fall into it, and his last thought was that San Benito, his one final connection to his theological education, had ultimately failed him.

Jacobo did not cry a single tear for all of these deaths until after Beatriz was interred in the Monsantillo mausoleum behind the parish church of Mangkono. During the entire funeral rites, from the Santa Misa, to the eulogies, which Consuela could not go through without breaking down in tears, and all throughout the short, slow walk from the church to the mausoleum, in which he shared the burden of bearing Beatriz's casket with Salvador, Silvestre, Amadeo Visbal and his son Angelo, and one sacristan, Jacobo did not cry. But when they all arrived back at the house at Hacienda Marianita, Jacobo sat in his chair and sobbed, for Paz, for Beatriz, and even for Selina, but most of all he cried for the children who were taken as punishment for sins committed by their parents. That night, when the multong vengativa did not bother Jacobo, he began to hope that perhaps he had been made to pay enough.

But the deaths did not stop at the third. Esperanza's baby was a stillborn, and although it was officially a Monsantillo, Margarita still held a ceremony in the house at Hacienda Marianita, and declared a state of mourning. Esperanza took this mourning to heart, but she mourned herself, not her baby, her mourning consisting of lashing out at Santa Rita in her prayers. That horrible woman granted her wish after all, but terribly, perversely late, as if she was mocking her. Esperanza refused to see any visitors in the hospital, and spoke only to Fe, the maid whom her mother sent to help care for her there. When she was discharged from the hospital, she requested to stay for a while at the house at Hacienda Marianita, but cloistered herself inside her old bedroom and refused to talk to anyone, except for Margarita.

'Hija, there will be another one,' Margarita said, sitting in a couch by the window in Esperanza's old bedroom. It was sunset, and a weak ray of light was streaming through the window to land on the foot of Esperanza's unmade bed.

'I don't know if I can, Mama,' Esperanza said.

'Of course, you can.'

'I meant I don't know if I want to.'

'Of course you want to.'

Esperanza, who was reclining in her bed, glared at her mother and let out an exaggerated sigh.

'Mama, you are overbearing.'

'You are young and you have your whole life ahead of you.'

'No I don't, because now there is Silvestre.'

'What now? You wanted him, didn't you?'

'I changed my mind.'

'Ay, dios mio, Esperanza!' Margarita threw up her hands and stood up from the chair. 'You had us all fooled!'

'I was certainly not fooling anyone, Mama.'

'But this is too soon! Change your mind and be sad after you are married ten years. Not now. The flowers from your wedding bouquet have not even completely wilted yet.'

'But when they have, am I allowed to change my mind then?' Esperanza said wryly.

'Stop that sarcasm.' Margarita turned her back on Esperanza and went to the window. She could see four of the bodyguards milling about from below. She knew that two bodyguards were assigned to her by Jacobo, but as she had not left the house since Paz's funeral, and had no plans to leave the innumerable, misshapen walls of her house, she had no idea which of these men was supposed to keep her alive. Behind her, Esperanza, reclining in bed, her body still misshapen and exhausted, contemplated her fate and began to suspect that there was nothing more for her after this, and she felt isolated in her disappointment. She felt that her mother would never understand, and Sofia, who she almost never talked to any more, much more so. She felt a deep sob forming in her chest, which slowly rose into her throat like a giant bubble that felt like it was choking her, and she could not breathe so she inadvertently opened her mouth and grimaced, her face contorting in a pain that wasn't anywhere in her body but was everywhere in her soul.

Chapter 14

Flowers for the Children

Assumpta started seeing a ghost on the morning of her ninth birthday. At first, she thought it was just her broken vision playing optical tricks on her, but she had tested her eyes twice since that morning. She tried to imitate her ophthalmologist's tests by reading from the calendar that hung on the wall of Jacobo's office, while she stood with her back against the opposite wall. She took off her eye patch from her right eye, which had gone completely blind, and trained her vision on to the writing on the calendar, which she could see very clearly with her left eye. She covered her right eye with her right hand and began reading the calendar.

'*Agosto, mil novecientos cincuenta y ocho,*' she said loudly to the empty room. '*Fecha uno. Fecha dos. Fecha tres. Fecha cuatro. Fecha cinco.*' Her Spanish pronunciation has been improving according to Mrs Palacio, but she knew it was still not as smooth as Inez's, who could prattle off to Jacobo at a thousand words a minute.

She continued reading until the first half of the month. '*Fecha quince, Fiesta de la Asuncion de la Santisima Virgen Maria.*' And then she laughed a little when she saw the next box on the calendar. The number sixteen was printed on the calendar but the words underneath it were written in Jacobo's hand. '*Fecha dieciseis, cumpleaño de Assumpta.*'

Then she put her eye patch back on over her right eye and continued reading. '*Fecha diecinueve, Fiesta del Cumpleaño de Manuel L. Quezon. Fecha veintenueve, Dia de los Heroes Nacionales.*' Then she realized that she had aspirated a letter that she shouldn't have, and repeated the line. '*Fecha veintenueve, Dia de los Heroes Nacionales.*'

As she said the last word, she saw the same ghost from the corner of her left eye, which was the good eye. Slowly she turned her head to the left, but the ghost disappeared into the corner of two walls.

Assumpta, wanting to see if the ghost would reappear if the circumstances were exactly the same, looked at the calendar. 'Fecha diecinueve, Fiesta del Cumpleaño de Manuel L. Quezon. Fecha veintenueve, Dia de los Heroes Nacionales,' she said, deliberately failing to aspirate what she should have, and then saying it again a second time but correctly. 'Fecha veintenueve, Dia de los Heroes Nacionales.'

And then she waited for the ghost to reappear in the corner of her left vision, but it didn't. Assumpta walked to the corner of the wall where the ghost disappeared, and knocked, and then waited for something to happen. When nothing happened, she went back to her spot, and continued her vision test.

'*Fecha veinte. Fecha veinte uno. Fecha veinte dos. Fecha veinte tres.*'

At the moment Jacobo walked into his office, right into Assumpta's full front view.

'Papa!'

'*Chiquitin*, what are you doing here?' Jacobo said, taking his seat behind the desk.

'I was testing my vision, Papa.'

'What were you reading?'

'That calendar.' Assumpta pointed, and then went to sit on the chair in front of Jacobo's desk, the one for his business-related visitors.

'Are you ready for your birthday?'

'Yes, Papito!'

'Bien!'

Assumpta twisted her neck a little bit so that the corner of the room where she saw the ghost would be in the corner of her left eye, hoping that she would see it again, but she didn't.

This year, there was no party for Assumpta's birthday, in keeping with the ongoing mourning period for Paz, and the two other families were also in mourning for their own departed kin. But there was a nice luncheon in the dining room for just the Arguelleses, and a birthday cake for Assumpta. It was Mrs Palacio who went to town to order the birthday cake on behalf of Margarita, who refused to leave the house since Paz's funeral. Assumpta, quite tired of wearing full black outfits every day, even though it was for Paz, requested an all-white cake, and Mrs Palacio, unfamiliar with such things, did not want the cake to look like a wedding cake, so she asked the baker to refrain from using lace and flowers as decoration, and explained Assumpta's favourite things as best as she could to the baker, and so when the cake was eventually delivered, it was indeed all white. It was a rectangular single-layer fondant cake and decorated with marzipans that were carefully shaped into books, stacks of paper, shrubbery with tiny leaves, and a tiny Assumpta-shaped figurine, also all-white, with curly hair, an eye patch, and wearing a dress with short, ruffled sleeves and a ruffled hem. The baker innovated by glazing everything with a pearlized finish, to comply with the strict colour request without sacrificing dimension and effect. Assumpta was delighted and ran to embrace Mrs Palacio's waist, while Margarita nodded at the old woman in approval. For candles, there were nine short ones shaped like fountain pens, uncapped and with nibs pointing up, and one taller candle in the shape of a capped pen. Jacobo lit the nine shorter candles, everyone sang 'Cumpleaños Feliz', and Assumpta blew out the candles. Then Margarita lit the tenth candle.

Assumpta closed her eyes, said her birthday wish out loud, 'I wish to see more. Por favor. Muchas gracias,' opened her eyes, and blew out the tenth candle. In the corner of her left eye she could see the ghost again, for the fourth time since that morning. Then she wondered if birthday wishes were truly granted, as her wish last year did not seem to have been.

Later, when the entire house was supposed to be having siesta, she stayed up in her room, waiting to see if she would see the ghost again. The room had already been redecorated after Paz's funeral. The two beds were taken into storage, and a new, larger bed was brought in for Assumpta and placed in the centre of what used to be the space in between the two smaller beds that used to be there. It felt awkward to Assumpta, and not just because she felt like she could drown in a bed that big. It was largely because she had always shared that room with Paz, even if she didn't share much of her thoughts with her, as Assumpta thought her sister lacked imagination and preferred to merely give exactly what she was expected to give in anything, be it school, family, religious devotion, eating her vegetables, or sleeping. Paz could fall asleep at will and wake up at will, Assumpta thought, unlike herself, who had always considered the requirement of sleep a nuisance, and then her thoughts of Paz turned into thoughts of her old secret room with the claw-foot bathtub, no longer a secret since the day Paz died. She wondered if someone else had been in that room since that day. She decided to go and have a look.

Nothing had been disturbed in Assumpta's secret room which was no longer a secret, so she assumed that no one had been inside since the last time she was there. The moment she walked in, she could smell all of the fear, the uncertainty, the gunpowder, Margarita's perfume, that wafted around in the air the night Paz died. She walked to the claw-foot bathtub, retrieved the old briefcase, placed it on the concrete floor like she always had, and opened it. There was some feeling of familiarity to the action, as this had been a happy place for her for several months; this room could never feel sinister to her, as it had sheltered her, her mother, her brother, and Mrs Palacio, from certain death. But being in this room and holding the old briefcase again after everything that had happened no longer held the same feeling for Assumpta. She closed her one good eye and tried to remember the days when she used to be so intent on mapping the strange rooms and corridors of the house, in the hopes of figuring out the mysteries behind the strange proportions of the spaces, and could no longer feel the same urge. She tried to feel beneath her feet, to see if the house still heaved, but she could feel nothing. The house was no longer the same, this room was no longer the same, and without that feeling of being part of something enchanted, Assumpta felt that it was time for her to leave this room behind.

She took the old briefcase up to her bedroom, which she no longer shared with Paz, and hid it under her bed, like she used to do before she found her secret room, and that did not feel the same as it used to either. Without being enveloped in her usual cloud of fascination, Assumpta felt lost, lost without Paz, lost without her right eye, lost without her maps, lost without Sebastian's papers. She went back to bed for her supposed siesta, and when she could not go to sleep, her hands went underneath her pillow where she had been keeping her pearl rosary, and she let her mind wander from Paz to Mercedes, who had given her that very rosary exactly a year ago on her eighth birthday.

'*Donde esta usted, abuelita?*' Assumpta whispered into the quiet afternoon. 'Where are you?'

On a different afternoon Jacobo went to see Salvador in the house at Hacienda Vida. He had been thinking about Paz and Beatriz, Beatriz more than Paz, but only because he felt that he really had done nothing for her while she was still alive. He had not even visited her when she was ill, perhaps because he did not want a reminder of his neglect, not that he was under any legal obligation to her, but knowing that he had neglected his moral duties to her and that now he would never see her again drove a tiny pinprick through his shrivelled, hardened, blackened heart.

So he went to see Salvador, who received him in his office beside the sala.

'Compadre!' Salvador stood up from behind his desk and met Jacobo quickly as he was halfway through the door. 'What a nice surprise. Please, have a seat, have a seat.'

Then he himself went to the door and called out to a passing maid, 'Bituin, bring us coffee and *ibos.*'

Salvador was slightly nervous at the sudden and unannounced visit, because he was only very much aware of just how much money he owed Jacobo, which, although he was not scheduled to pay back yet, was always on the forefront of his mind. He could not figure out Jacobo's mood, as the man's countenance had grown to be increasingly inscrutable, but Salvador's accounting ledgers were always updated, so he knew he was ready for answers in case Jacobo did come to ask for a payment.

'How is the family?' Salvador asked.

'Bien. The family is fine,' Jacobo said. He thought of asking about Consuela, but quickly changed his mind, and then to rid himself of the awkward feeling, he went straight to the point. 'I would like to build a greenhouse on your property in memory of Beatriz.'

Salvador looked at him blankly for an entire minute.

'Pick an area, anywhere in your hacienda, and I will build the greenhouse there,' Jacobo continued, his face still completely inexpressive to Salvador.

But just then, Bituin came into the room bearing a tray with two cups of coffee, two saucers of ibos, a small container of sugar, silver forks, glasses of water and napkins. She went to the small table at the corner of Salvador's office and set it for two.

Salvador sighed quietly in relief at the interruption, and then invited Jacobo to transfer to the table.

'A greenhouse, compadre?' Salvador asked after Bituin had left.

'Yes. Consider it a gift from me. I have not done anything for your family in these difficult times.' Jacobo picked up a fork, cut a piece of ibos, and popped it into his mouth.

'But you have, compadre,' Salvador was quick to assure him. 'You certainly have, and it's been keeping the hacienda afloat while I am implementing the solutions to those wretched problems from last year.'

'That was for the hacienda, but this is for family,' Jacobo said. 'That was for money and security. This is for love.' He picked up his cup of coffee and took a sip, not looking at Salvador.

Salvador was slightly taken aback, for this must have been the very first time that he had ever heard Jacobo use the word, but some part of him instantly understood where his compadre was. Jacobo had lost his own daughter when he was the one who was supposed to be killed, and so he was projecting his grief towards memorializing Beatriz. Salvador remembered how Beatriz looked during that final Christmas Noche Buena, gaunt but happy, her black, curly hair standing out from the heads of his other children with their straight brown tresses. That was the last time he heard his daughter laugh, and this memory compelled him to accept Jacobo's gift.

'Compadre, I am already in your debt and you certainly don't need to be giving us anything more, but I accept this gift wholeheartedly and with much gratitude, for Beatriz.'

'Bueno!' Jacobo said. 'That's final then. Now please eat. This ibos is very good.'

'This ibos is from Albay, brought over by Salvacion just the other day,' Salvador said, referring to his household cook. 'She went to visit her mother there, and her mother made these and sent these over for us.'

Jacobo nodded, smiling thinly. He could appreciate the loyalty of generations of servants, but this only reminded him that his own hacienda has been lacking in loyal servants for a while, and he had been the last to know about it. But he shook off the feeling quickly, because he already knew what to do about that problem.

The coffee and ibos paved the way for their conversation to veer towards much safer subjects, which included Salvador's plans to merge one of his abaca plantations with one of the abaca plantations of Manuel Visbal to provide Hacienda Vida with operational and logistical support in solving the dampness problems of his abaca storage. Jacobo's generous loan ensured that Salvador would be able to stand on equal footing with Manuel in this merge. Salvador sounded hopeful, and Jacobo was pleased, although no one would ever see it on his face as he finished eating his ibos in such an impenetrable way.

It was Consuela who decided where the greenhouse was to be built. When Salvador told her about Jacobo's visit, Consuela looked him straight in the eyes silently for a full two minutes, and then said, 'Beside our house, facing the east wall.'

Consuela decided, quite uncharacteristically, that she wanted to head the entire project, and she did not explain why, but everyone just assumed it was her way of mourning her daughter, who went to sleep for months without waking, with an assortment of flowers growing over her. Salvador, busy with the hacienda and the merger, and aware that his wife needed comfort that he somehow could not give, let her be.

The foreman for the project suggested that, because of the vindictive storms of Camarines, the foundation would have to be made of reinforced concrete and buried much deeper than usual. The glass panels might end up shattering, but those would be easy to replace if the foundation and the steel frame and trusses were sturdy enough. Consuela agreed and decided that the greenhouse would be ten feet wide by twenty feet long, and, in defiance of the storms that she was certain would always come, sixteen feet tall. She also decided that the entire structure would be angled to be squarely facing Beatriz's bedroom windows. When she shared the plan with Salvador, in his mind he appreciated the symbolism, but didn't mention it. Consuela, however, was the only person who knew that the greenhouse wasn't a gift but a plea for forgiveness funded by Jacobo, so the positioning of the greenhouse was meant as an apology, a form of atonement, a kneeling in front of Beatriz. It was a grand, final, dreadfully belated, and utterly useless gesture of reparation from both Jacobo and Consuela, as was the tradition of these families who never actually apologize for anything, but project their torment on to their houses and their lands, Jacobo most especially.

Through the east window of the bedroom that she continued to share with Silvestre in the house at Hacienda Vida, Esperanza saw Beatriz's greenhouse rise. At first, the flowers were dug up from the flower beds and carefully transferred to pots by their gardeners. Then large stones and steel bars were laid in a grid on the ground and covered with concrete, with more steel bars rising to about a foot high, and which were eventually covered with concrete to form a low bounding wall. Then the steel frame was put in, first the walls and then the rafters, dull metallic grey lines standing against the sunlight of the morning like a defiant skeleton, all of which were eventually painted white. The clear glass panels were installed last and were held in place by putty and metal clips. The door to the greenhouse was also panelled in clear class, and over that door, in a triangular shape, was the only coloured part of the whole structure, a vibrant stained-glass piece dominated by blue shards that formed the letter B. Consuela felt there was no need for the full initials, as no one in Camarines needed any reminder of whom this land belonged to. Esperanza, seeing everything through a new, growing habit of outward silence and aloofness, cried invisibly for the death of her own dreams, for which monuments could not be built.

The house at Hacienda Marianita would also have its own monument for its own fallen daughter. Jacobo had the lounge on the second floor opened up again, which he had ordered sealed shut after Paz had died in it, but this time he had most of its external wall torn down, and its floor extended and tiled, supported by new pillars on the ground, to make a wide balcony with a view of the sunset. On the side of this balcony was a staircase that led to a new rooftop garden, decorated with a profusion of potted plants bearing multi-coloured blooms. The potted plants lined the sides of the rooftop garden, concealing the high railings and most of the steel frame that rose over two of the walls, which were panelled in glass to act as windbreakers, not just for the plants but for the people who did not want their hair ruffled or their outfits blown askew. On the farthest wall, a small bronze plaque, bearing only the words 'En Memoria de Paz', was mounted. Above everything was a trellised roof, empty when new, but would, over the decades as the Arguelleses lived on in the constantly transmogrified house at Hacienda Marianita where there was blood under the eternally green and always precisely cut grass, also become home to flowering vines that would bloom only when an Arguelles was about to have a new secret.

Margarita considered the new rooftop garden as part of the outside of the house, and never stepped foot in it, in keeping with her decision to never leave the house after Paz's funeral. Jacobo, who had ordered it built, only climbed the stairs to inspect the ongoing work and to approve the finished work, and never returned. Jacobo II and Inez, however, found great enjoyment in the rooftop garden, and spent many hours there almost every day, in the wind and late afternoon sun, talking and having merienda while seated on the chairs closest to the glass walls, to prevent their food from being blown away by the strong Camarines wind.

'On Wednesday, I want to ride to the hills with Toriano and Basilio the encargado. We will return home in the evening. Come with us,' Inez said, then showed a large forkful of suman with latik into her mouth.

'Did Papa allow you to go?'

'I haven't told him yet. He can send additional guards with us if that will make him more comfortable about us going.'

'Do you really have to go, especially after what happened?'

'What happened was that I defended myself single-handedly with a bolo. And now I am allowed to have both a bolo and a rifle, for even better defence.'

'I don't know, Inez. Maybe you shouldn't be going out there too soon, at least while Papa hasn't solved the problem yet,' Jacobo II said, sipping his coffee.

'I take it you're not coming,' Inez said, pointedly looking at him.

'No. And I don't think you should go, either.'

'I know why you think I shouldn't, but if I mope around inside the house for any longer like Mama, those people will begin to think we have been cowered.'

'I don't think they believe we have been cowered,' Jacobo II said.

'Why? What do you know that Papa hasn't told me?'

Jacobo II put his head close to Inez's and told her.

In the few months that had passed since the fire and the bloody invasion of the house at Hacienda Marianita, Jacobo had made executive changes. He attributed his continuing survival only partly to his own grit and strategic thinking, but felt that it was largely the powers of destiny that allowed him to survive. He believed that he did not deserve the peace of death, and so he had to endure the deaths of Paz, and then of Beatriz, and even of Mercedes who simply disappeared. He knew there would be others who would die before he did, and that he would be the last Arguelles left alive, ancient, decrepit, unsuitable for the reward of death, his bones clattering about this empty, monstrous, heaving house. He knew, as the multong vengativa had made it clear with her enraged eyes, that he would forever be burdened with the punishment of life and see the people he loved die around him.

Nevertheless, Jacobo was still an Arguelles to the core, and he knew himself well enough to conclude that out of all his sins, one sin he would never be accused of was that of abandoning his post as current head of the clan. So he continued his duties to the hacienda and to his family, two entities that existed separately at the beginning but over the decades had become inextricably melded to each other, the misfortune of one directly becoming the misfortune of the other. He had decided to involve Jacobo II more deeply in the affairs of the hacienda, to train him as he should go. However, while Jacobo II was still finishing up his formal education at the seminario, he assigned Inez as a steward for Jacobo II's eventual role. Both Jacobo and Margarita had decided that Inez and Assumpta were to stop going to school for the time being, so Jacobo was free to train

Inez on the operational affairs of the hacienda. Inez, out of her months of proximity to her own resolute, cold-hearted father, began to become resolute and cold-hearted herself, but unlike Jacobo, she remained fearless, which was an even more deadly combination.

That afternoon on the rooftop garden, as Jacobo II sat with his head close to Inez's, telling her what Jacobo had told him, Guadalupe was in the living room on the first floor of the house, checking if the curtains needed to be washed. She heard every single word that Jacobo II told Inez, very clearly, over the sound of the heaving of the house. By instinct her hand went to the pocket of her purple dress, to clutch her rosary.

Assumpta, who was nine years old but also older, could not hear like Guadalupe and was not fearless as Inez, but in her single-eyed vision, could finally begin to see, or so she thought, in her limited understanding of life and the world, which did not yet extend beyond Camarines. For days she draw new maps of the house and had even extended her activities to pulling out some of the huge, old maps from the map drawers in Jacobo's library, rolling them for easier carrying, and then hauling them to her room and unrolling them on the floor. Her new, large bed had since been pushed against one of the walls of her bedroom, which was done by three maids upon a request that she placed with Mrs Palacio, and this freed up ample space on the floor for her to unroll the maps, which she slipped, unrolled, underneath her bed for hiding, just as she did the old briefcase of hand-drawn maps just a little over a year before.

One late night, when the house was dark and quiet and everyone was in bed, Assumpta had a flicker of a memory. There was something she had read in Sebastian's papers months ago that she did not pay attention to, but she had an idea what it could probably mean. She got out of bed and turned on the light. She took the old briefcase from underneath her bed, took out the cut-up pieces that used to be Sebastian's papers, laid them all out on the floor, and began putting together the little pieces of paper that were irregularly shaped. Beneath her the house, the repository of secrets and blood, heaved very gently. All this time, the house and its ghosts, who knew everything, every word uttered, every secret kept, every nook and cranny of the house, every turn of the screw that caused the wheel to pivot, had been telling them things, but no one paid enough attention to what the house had been trying to say. Even the guidance of the maps and letters fell on obtuse hearts that were totally devoid of insight. The Arguelleses chose to favour their warm beds and full stomachs and pleasant conversation over facing the horrors of the past, even to the point of physically building over the past with their monuments and their strange rooms. Theirs was a past that was never really past but lived on in the present, in the house, in their monuments, in the voices that passed from room to room, in the vapours and aromas that floated over the heads of the oblivious.

While putting together the pieces that she had cut apart just months ago, Assumpta felt herself being transported back to that one night with the thunderstorm when she first told Paz about the maps and Paz said she was crazy. On the table in front of her there were flowers growing on the little pieces of paper, their roots as fine as hair, wrapped around each piece of secret.

Acknowledgements

They say that writing is a very isolated job. While that is generally true, the isolation is not absolute. I did write the words of this novel myself, but many people have also been instrumental in how this novel has emerged in its final form.

The first 6,000 words of this novel were subjected to the workshop circuit in August 2021, under the 60th University of the Philippines National Writers' Workshop. My co-fellows gave me not only important suggestions on how to make the draft better and the general idea for the novel more grounded, but also gave me moral support and friendship. I am grateful for Erik Guzman Pingol, Louyzza Maria Victoria Vasquez, Edward Perez, Maria Amparo N. Warren, Amado Anthony G. Mendoza III, Napoleon Arcilla III, Layeta Bucoy, Ma. Cecilia Dela Rosa, Alexandra Alcasid, Adrian Ho, and Joel Donato Jacob.

The panellists to the 60th UPNWW have been just as helpful. Many thanks to Professors Gemino Abad, Virgilio Almario, Romulo Baquiran, Luna Sicat-Cleto, Jose Y. Dalisay, Jr., Eugene Y. Evasco, J. Neil Garcia, Vladimeir B. Gonzales, Ramon Guillermo, Cristina Pantoja Hidalgo, Vim Nadera, Charlson J. Ong, Jun Cruz Reyes, Anna Felicia C. Sanchez, and Rolando B. Tolentino.

I am also deeply grateful to Joel Pablo Salud, Victor Dennis Nierva, and John Ray Hontanar, who read parts of this novel while I was working on it. Thank you as well to Louella E. Fortez and Rogelio Braga for hashing out with me the literary theories connected to the issues discussed in this novel. I appreciate them all, most especially their friendship.

Special thanks must be given to Professor Danton Remoto for encouraging me to finish writing this novel.

I also thank my father, Eduardo, who kept himself open to all of my questions regarding life in their old home, and for helping me with details and facts to the best of his knowledge. Thank you as well to his siblings for their stories about the old hacienda in Mical Bical, now long gone, but still alive in their memory. To Margarita, Inez, Salvador, Sebastian, Emmanuel, Wilfredo, Andres, and Sarah, I am very grateful.

There must be special mention of their mother, my grandmother, Francisca Kare viuda de Moll, who held on to all the photographs from the 1920s to the 1970s. They were already turning silver at the edges, but they held the details that I was able to describe in the novel. I would have loved to know what she thinks about what I have written, but she is no longer with us.

I thank my cousin Edward Recto for propelling this novel forward with his research on the genealogy of our families, and for being the guardian of all the family stories, happy and sad, official and unofficial.

I also thank my cousin Michelle Moll for reminding me of details from our childhood that, due to my failing memory, would have been buried forever, but will now live on in this novel.

Certain people also took things off my plate and away from my mental and emotional zone, so I could concentrate on finishing the writing of this novel. If not for what they did, fuelled by their acceptance of what I had to do and their faith in my abilities, this novel would have remained unfinished.

Professors Jose Wendell Capili and Ruth Pison allowed me to temporarily leave my graduate thesis behind so I can focus on finishing writing this novel. They never questioned me, never even required an explanation. Their magnanimity is astounding, and I will always strive to be worthy of it.

Atty. Angel R. Ojastro III took on all of the worries, pressures, and stresses connected to my legal battles so that I will be free to do the things I would never have been able to do otherwise.

My parents, Eduardo and Eden, provided absolutely everything that I needed, from allowing me to live in their house, with not just one but two bedrooms, both exclusively for me, down to the everyday coffee and tea. Their generosity is beyond measure. Yaya Emely Aras also took very good care of me, making sure I had food to eat and that my clothes were washed and my floors were swept.

My sister Mary Francis Moll and her daughter Francesca Maye Moll took on the concerns of my son so that I would be temporarily free of motherly duties, this on top of my sister's largesse that prevented me from worrying about my personal finances. My son, Chandler Patrick Yuboco, gave me the mental space, and still always reminded me to eat. My dear Jawaid Razon Banaag kept me physically healthy despite my strange hours and very sedentary days and nights, and he accepted my frenzied, manic, baffling progress. My brother, Mario Eduardo Moll, fielded everything else that might have come my way to potentially disturb my creative process.

I would also like to express my gratitude to two different writing programmes that helped me sustain my goals and deadlines for this novel. I wrote the first 50,000 words of this novel during the entire month of November 2012 under the National Novel Writing Month challenge. I finished writing the rest of this novel and all of its major edits during the Clarion West Write-A-Thon of 2022.

Finally, many thanks to Nora Nazerene Abu Bakar for deciding to take a chance with this novel and give it to readers living beyond my familiar shores, and to my editor, Amberdawn Manaois, for her patience and intuitiveness in dealing with my failings as a writer.

A decade spans my process of writing this novel. I devoted only thirty days to it in 2012, and did not really add anything to it until 2022. Within the decade that the novel remained in limbo, its future uncertain, a significant part of my life happened. It was a life that helped me write the final ending that now seals this novel's fate. For that decade lived, I am also grateful.